RAMPAGE

A Delta Force Unleashed Thriller

Also by J. Robert Kennedy

James Acton Thrillers

The Protocol	*The Riddle*	*The Cylon Curse*
Brass Monkey	*Blood Relics*	*The Viking Deception*
Broken Dove	*Sins of the Titanic*	*Keepers of the Lost Ark*
The Templar's Relic	*Saint Peter's Soldiers*	*The Tomb of Genghis Khan*
Flags of Sin	*The Thirteenth Legion*	*The Manila Deception*
The Arab Fall	*Raging Sun*	*The Fourth Bible*
The Circle of Eight	*Wages of Sin*	*Embassy of the Empire*
The Venice Code	*Wrath of the Gods*	*Armageddon*
Pompeii's Ghosts	*The Templar's Revenge*	*No Good Deed*
Amazon Burning	*The Nazi's Engineer*	*The Last Soviet*
	Atlantis Lost	

Special Agent Dylan Kane Thrillers

Rogue Operator	*Black Widow*	*State Sanctioned*
Containment Failure	*The Agenda*	*Extraordinary Rendition*
Cold Warriors	*Retribution*	*Red Eagle*
Death to America		*The Messenger*

Templar Detective Thrillers

The Templar Detective	*The Sergeant's Secret*	*The Black Scourge*
The Parisian Adulteress	*The Unholy Exorcist*	*The Lost Children*
	The Code Breaker	

Kriminalinspektor Wolfgang Vogel Mysteries

The Colonel's Wife	*Sins of the Child*

Delta Force Unleashed Thrillers

Payback	*The Lazarus Moment*	*The Cuban Incident*
Infidels	*Kill Chain*	*Rampage*
	Forgotten	

Detective Shakespeare Mysteries

Depraved Difference	*Tick Tock*	*The Redeemer*

Zander Varga, Vampire Detective

The Turned

RAMPAGE

A Delta Force Unleashed Thriller

J. ROBERT KENNEDY

UnderMill PRESS

Copyright ©2021 J. Robert Kennedy

ISBN: 9781990418235

First Edition

For the doctors, nurses, and support staff who ended my misery, and quite possibly saved my life.

RAMPAGE

A Delta Force Unleashed Thriller

"If you prick us do we not bleed? If you tickle us do we not laugh? If you poison us do we not die? And if you wrong us shall we not revenge?"

The Merchant of Venice, Act 3, Scene 1
William Shakespeare

"It is impossible to suffer without making someone pay for it; every complaint already contains revenge."

Friedrich Nietzsche

PREFACE

In America, rival gangs battle for turf on a daily basis, the collateral damage incalculable. The Russian mob is one of the most brutal. With an estimated 250,000 members spread over fifty countries, and affiliates numbering as many as three million, they are involved in all manner of criminal activity including human trafficking, racketeering, drug trafficking, extortion, arms trafficking, gambling, prostitution, pornography, and much more.

Fortune Magazine estimates the Russian mob brings in over $8.5 billion per year, and they vigorously protect their territory. The United Nations recently estimated that between 2000-2017, mafias around the world were responsible for over one million deaths, with the Russian mob responsible for many of those.

And should someone witness one of their many crimes, threatening their operation, they wouldn't hesitate to protect themselves.

In the most violent way imaginable.

Person Street

Fayetteville, North Carolina

"I think we made a mistake with those bridesmaid dresses," said Maggie Harris as she fumbled for her keys. "They're absolutely hideous. I can't make you guys wear those."

"They're not so bad." Shirley Belme held out a hand. "Give me those."

Maggie smiled gratefully and handed over her bags then successfully retrieved the keys, holding them up triumphantly. "Found them!" She wagged the fob at Shirley. "They're hideous and you know it."

Vanessa Moore held up her phone with a photo of the dress in question. "I don't know, it's not so bad."

Maggie stopped and gave her a look. "Hideous."

Vanessa giggled. "You're right, they are completely hideous, but they're supposed to be. They're meant to make you the most beautiful woman in the room. All eyes should be on you, not the bridesmaids. Remember when Will and Kate got married? Everyone was talking about Pippa's booty. If she had been wearing some god-awful pastel-colored thing, nobody would have noticed,

2

but her dress was beautiful, so the whole world was talking about her can and not how beautiful Kate looked."

Maggie eyed her. "I don't really remember that."

Vanessa tapped at her phone then held up a photo.

Maggie whistled. "Wow, that *is* a nice ass."

Joanne Lightman leaned in. "I'd switch teams."

Vanessa laughed. "But if she had some foam-green dress on, nobody would have been looking and Joanne wouldn't be questioning her sexuality."

Everyone roared with laughter and Maggie, feeling a little better, continued toward the SUV. It was late, the sun just setting. They had taken far longer than planned picking out the dresses, but no one was complaining. It had been a blast. She was elated that the wedding plans were finally moving forward again. Soon, she'd be marrying the love of her life and she couldn't wait. He was the best man she had ever met in her life, and she loved him so much, she couldn't wait to start their life together.

And an afternoon out with her friends that stretched into the evening was just what she had needed. She paused at the rear of the vehicle. "Anybody want to grab dinner?"

Heads bobbed all around as she pressed the button to open the rear hatch. Everyone loaded their purchases inside and she was about to close the trunk when somebody cried out. They all fell silent, staring about for the source. The parking lot of the strip mall was mostly empty, and no one was in sight.

Thuds followed another cry.

"What is that?" asked Shirley.

Vanessa held a finger to her lips. "I think somebody's getting beaten."

"Are you sure?"

3

Another cry and Vanessa hissed, "We need to get the hell out of here."

Maggie was aghast at the idea. "We can't just leave. We have to help."

Vanessa vehemently shook her head. "Listen, I grew up in bad neighborhoods. You mind your own business, or you get yourself killed. Let's get in the car, get on the road, then we'll call 9-1-1 and let the police deal with it."

Footfalls pounded in an alleyway just to their right, separating the strip mall they were just in and a Wendy's. A man emerged and they all gasped as his face was revealed by the streetlights, bloodied and swollen. He turned and spotted them, stretching a hand toward them.

"Help! Please help!"

Shirley yelped and Vanessa slammed the trunk closed. "Everybody get in, now!"

But no one moved, all too shocked to react.

Two men rushed out of the alleyway, one with a gun held out in front of him. He squeezed the trigger twice, the muzzle flashing in the dim light, and the beaten man cried out then collapsed.

Vanessa hauled open the back passenger side door of the SUV and grabbed Shirley. "We have to go now!" she cried. She shoved her into the back seat and slammed the door shut, rushing back around as the men noticed them. Once of them smiled and walked toward them as the other fired another shot into the victim's head, the body jerking on the ground one final time. Vanessa grabbed the keys out of Maggie's hand, startling her. Vanessa opened the rear door and pushed Maggie and Joanne toward it as she hauled open the driver-side door and leaped inside.

The smiling man raised his own weapon as Vanessa started the engine. Maggie snapped out of her stunned panic and grabbed Joanne, hauling her toward the open rear door. The man fired and Joanne gasped then collapsed to the ground. Maggie screamed and ducked behind the door. She darted out and grabbed Joanne under the arms, dragging her with all of her might as another shot rang out, slamming into the rear of the vehicle. She lifted her friend up, the dead weight making it almost impossible, and with one last roar of effort, she tumbled her into the rear seat.

The man fired several times at Vanessa, the side window shattering as everyone inside cried out. Maggie stepped toward the door as Shirley pulled Joanne out of the way to make room. Another shot fired, taking out the rear passenger window. Maggie winced as something hit her arm and she tumbled backward, smacking the pavement hard as both men fired on them.

"Go!" she screamed as she made eye contact with the crouching Vanessa. Vanessa's eyes filled with tears as she shook her head. "Go, or they'll kill us all!"

Vanessa maintained eye contact for another moment then closed her eyes, tears rolling down her cheeks. "I'm so sorry." She put the vehicle in gear and hammered on the gas, Shirley screaming for her to stop. Maggie watched from the ground as the SUV leaped over the curb and onto the street, a hail of gunfire following it, then breathed a sigh of relief as the shots stopped, her friends escaping. She turned her head as the footfalls approached, and the smiling man pointed a gun directly at her head. She squeezed her eyes shut, unwilling to stare at death, and as her life flashed before her eyes, one image dominated.

The smiling face of the man she loved.

And the man she prayed would avenge her death.

Delta Force operator Command Sergeant Major Burt "Big Dog" Dawson.

Vanessa struggled to control the SUV. The wheel violently yanked out of her hands as they bounced over the curb then the center median. Cries from the back seat were ignored as she grabbed the steering wheel and battled to regain control. Gunfire continued behind them and she hammered her foot down, shoving the accelerator into the floor as they surged away from the scene of the crime. The gunfire stopped and she sat up, checking the rearview mirror to see one of the gunmen pointing his weapon toward the ground, Maggie lying helplessly on the pavement facing her executioner.

Alone.

A bus drove past in the opposite direction, blocking her view. Something flashed and she closed her eyes for a moment, certain it was the muzzle flash of a weapon firing. She opened her eyes and slowed down slightly.

"We have to get to a hospital!" cried Shirley. "Joanne's bleeding badly!"

Vanessa clasped the steering wheel as she battled the shock threatening to overwhelm her. "Call 9-1-1!"

Shirley reached into her purse, her hands trembling as Vanessa noticed the car was paired with a phone. Maggie must have put her purse in the back with her bags. She activated the voice feature and dialed 9-1-1 herself as Shirley continued to panic. The emergency operator answered immediately, and she reached back and grabbed Shirley's hand, squeezing to calm her friend's nerves.

And her own.

"Call the guys. They'll know what to do."

Shirley agreed and Vanessa turned her attention to the operator as she guided them toward the closest hospital.

And prayed Joanne survived.

1st Special Forces Operational Detachment—Delta HQ

Fort Bragg, North Carolina

A.k.a. "The Unit"

"I'm telling you, I don't order them anymore. The last time I did, there was absolutely no damn cheese," said Sergeant Carl "Niner" Sung. "What the hell is a breakfast burrito without cheese?"

"It's called McDogFood for a reason. I don't know how you can eat that shit," said Sergeant Leon "Atlas" James, his impossibly deep voice rumbling across the table as the Delta Force's Bravo Team assembled for a debrief after the latest op. They were America's elite warriors, members of 1st Special Forces Operational Detachment—Delta. The best of the best. They were brothers in arms, comrades, but they were also friends. They were Non-Commissioned Officers that did everything together professionally, and personally. Outside of their command structure, only their wives knew what they did for a living, though Atlas' girlfriend Vanessa Moore had been read in, and Niner's new girlfriend, Angela Henwood, had figured it out.

Beyond the dozen men in this room, the extended family included spouses, girlfriends, and children. And everyone here would lay down his life without hesitation to protect the others and their loved ones. They were tighter than most civilians could understand, the bond going beyond blood.

Niner gave his best friend the stink eye. "You're talking about an American institution, my friend. Mind your tongue or I might start to question your patriotism."

Sergeant Will "Spock" Lightman cocked an eyebrow. "If patriotism is measured in what we say about our fast-food restaurants, then I'm not sure if this country's worth protecting anymore."

Master Sergeant Mike "Red" Belme shook his shaved head that hid his natural ginger hair. "This country's always worth saving, even if McDogFood's burritos now suck."

Command Sergeant Major Burt "Big Dog" Dawson leaned back in his chair, folding his arms. "Oh, I don't know if they suck. The last time I had a breakfast burrito, it tasted fine to me."

Niner spun in his chair. "How many years ago was that?"

Dawson shrugged as he ran his fingers over his chiseled torso hidden beneath his shirt. "Does this body look like it eats fast food on a regular basis?"

"Amen, brother," commented the impossibly muscled Atlas, extending a fist to be bumped. Dawson leaned forward and completed the exchange as Spock yawned and checked his watch.

"It's not like the Colonel to be late."

Dawson agreed. "Something must be up."

Niner wasn't willing to let his rant go. "You know what the problem is? It's lack of consistency. You go there one day and the burrito is ice cold, the next day it's as if they microwaved it for five damn minutes and it's scalding hot. Some days there's lots of cheese, some there's no cheese, some there's hardly any. And don't get me started on the wrap. I swear they've changed something. It used to be like a white tortilla, but now it's some wholegrain thing. Tastes like shit, and sometimes it's hard as a rock. And don't get me started on how they wrap it. I thought that one of the great things about going to that restaurant was that whether you were in DC, London, or Beijing, it always tasted the same. Hell, you can go to the same restaurant, and when it comes to a burrito, it's completely different one minute to the next."

Atlas rolled his eyes. "There's a simple solution."

"What's that?"

"Stop getting it, then you won't be disappointed."

"But I like my burritos."

"Clearly you don't like *their* burritos."

"Yes, I do, when they get it right. I might have burritos there ten times in a row. One or two times it's perfection, but the other eight or nine times it sucks."

"So why punish yourself?"

Niner shrugged. "Angela asked me the same thing the last time we had breakfast together and I got another shit burrito. I think—"

The door burst open and their commanding officer, Colonel Thomas Clancy, rushed in. Everyone leaped to their feet before he could wave them off. They returned to their seats but Dawson remained standing as Clancy made eye contact, his expression revealing something horrible had happened.

That was when Dawson noticed the phone gripped in Clancy's hand.

The colonel closed the door. "Something's happened. Hold your questions. There's been an incident and I've already brought an ops center online to coordinate with the locals."

Dawson collapsed in his chair as Clancy continued to make eye contact with him.

"I'm going to give it to you straight. This is what we know. Maggie, Joanne, Shirley, and Vanessa left the dress shop less than fifteen minutes ago. A man was shot in the parking lot by two other men who then opened fire on Maggie and the others." He turned to Spock. "Joanne took a round."

Spock's jaw dropped, but words escaped him.

Dawson asked the question his friend couldn't. "Is she..."

"We don't know yet. She just arrived at the hospital. Three of them managed to get into the SUV and Vanessa got them out of there."

Three. And Vanessa drove, not Maggie.

Clancy faced Dawson. "Maggie was left behind."

Dawson gripped the arms of his chair, his knuckles turning white. "They left her there?"

"There was no choice, not from the situation that was described to me."

"So, what you're saying is—"

"I'm saying nothing. Police are still heading for the scene, and the ops center is pulling every camera feed we can to try to see what happened, but I have to tell you, Vanessa thinks she saw them shoot Maggie before she lost sight of her."

Dawson tore the arms off his chair then thrust to his feet, grabbing what remained and hurling it against the far wall. "Who's responsible?"

"We don't know." Clancy approached and put a hand on Dawson's shoulder. "But I promise you this, Sergeant Major, we're going to find out." He turned to Red. "Shirley is okay, so can you handle the debrief?"

Red nodded, the concern in his eyes for his friends evident. "Yes, sir."

"Good. Niner, you take BD to the scene of the attack. Atlas, you take Spock to the hospital. The rest of you, let's get this debrief out of the way, and then you're all on leave for one week."

Atlas helped the stunned Spock to his feet as Niner rose and led Dawson from the room. The four of them headed to the parking lot in silence, Dawson's mind a jumble of thoughts. Just when they were finally getting their lives back on track after the incident in Paris, now this. His chest ached and his stomach churned. He resisted the urge to vomit as he reached his Mustang and leaned against the cool metal. He squeezed his eyes shut, letting his anguish turn, a rage forming that turned from a growl to a roar as he slammed both fists on the hood.

He turned to the others. "We find out who did this then *we* deliver justice."

Spock stared at him, his jaw clenched. "We kill them all."

Atlas drew a breath, his massive chest expanding. "Every last one of them."

Cape Fear Valley Medical Center, Main Floor

Fayetteville, North Carolina

Atlas rushed up to the front desk at the hospital, shoving ahead of the gathered throng. "We're here to see a patient that was brought in with a gunshot wound. Her name is Joanne Lightman."

The nurse tapped at her computer. "Are you family?"

"I have her husband with me, Will Lightman."

The nurse pointed toward the elevator. "Fourth floor. ICU."

Atlas lowered his voice. "Is she…"

"Go to the fourth floor Nurses' Station. They'll let you know."

He turned and pointed toward the elevators, Spock following without comment. The ride here hadn't been long, though it had felt like an eternity, his irrational guilt gnawing at him in the silence with the knowledge Vanessa was unharmed. Yet was she? His years of experience on the battlefield told him the emotional scars she could suffer might run deeper than any physical. Calls had been made on the ride here and Spock's family was on the way, though they wouldn't be here for some time. For the moment, Atlas was Spock's support network until the rest of the team could get here after their debrief.

They rode up to the fourth floor, the elevator crowded. The doors opened and they stepped through, the Nurses' Station directly ahead.

"Atlas!"

He spun toward Vanessa's voice and held out his arms as she raced toward him. He embraced her, holding her tight, not saying anything as she sobbed in his arms. He let her go, remembering why he was here.

"Joanne?" asked Spock anxiously.

Vanessa reached out and took his hand in hers. "I'm so sorry, but I couldn't get her here in time."

The color drained from Spock's face. "Is she…"

Vanessa's shoulders slumped and her chin fell to her chest. "The bullet penetrated her stomach. She bled out in the car. I'm so sorry." She hugged him, his arms hanging loosely at his sides.

"Where is she?" His voice was barely a whisper.

Vanessa indicated a nearby room as she let him go. She stared up at him, her eyes wells of tears. "It happened quickly. She didn't suffer much." She pointed toward a doctor standing nearby. "That's her doctor. He can answer any questions you might have."

Atlas took his friend by the arm and led him toward the man, standing with another in a suit, a badge clipped to his belt indicating he was a detective.

Spock pulled toward the room. "I have to see her. Questions can wait."

A police officer stood by the door and held up a hand, blocking them. "I'm sorry, I can't let you in."

"This is her husband," explained Vanessa.

"I'm sorry, sir. I didn't realize." The officer stepped aside and Spock entered. Atlas followed but was stopped. "I'm sorry, sir, family only."

Atlas frowned but didn't protest, and as the door swung closed, his friend cried out, the wail filling the corridor, bringing everyone to a momentary halt.

And it gutted him.

He spotted a chair nearby and sat, battling to control his own emotions, asking himself the all-important questions.

Why?

And, more importantly, who?

En Route to Person Street

Fayetteville, North Carolina

Dawson and Niner drove in silence as they headed toward the crime scene, Dawson at the wheel of his prized 1964½ Mustang convertible in original poppy red. It had belonged to his father and had been handed down to him, the memories of the two of them working on it together cherished. He had hoped one day to pass it on to his own son, a son he was supposed to have with Maggie.

Supposed to have.

He gripped the steering wheel tight as he struggled to maintain control. There was still hope. There hadn't been any reports yet of her death. Niner's repeated calls to the police precinct handling the investigation only resulted in transfers to voicemail—whoever was assigned to the case wasn't taking calls.

But he'd know soon enough.

Niner pointed ahead, red and blue lights flashing, emergency vehicles blocking off the strip mall containing the small wedding boutique where Maggie and the others had spent the day. Police swarmed the area, and a gurney with a body bag on it was pushed toward a waiting coroner's vehicle.

Maggie.

His eyes burned and he closed them for a moment. The wheel jerked as Niner reached over and took control.

"Foot off the gas."

Dawson complied and opened his eyes. "I've got it." He pressed on the brakes gently, killing their speed, then guided them into the far end of the parking lot, the police having cordoned off the other side. He parked and shut off the engine, drawing a deep breath through his nose and holding it as he pushed against the steering wheel, forcing himself into the back of his seat. He exhaled loudly and let go, steeling for what was about to happen. He threw his door open and marched toward the crime scene, Niner at his side.

An officer held up a hand. "I'm afraid you can't come in here, sir."

Dawson pulled out his ID. "I'm Command Sergeant Major Dawson. I believe the victim is my fiancée, Mag—" His voice cracked.

"Maggie Harris," finished Niner, who also held up his ID. "I'm Sergeant Sung. We're both from the base. Our commanding officer, Colonel Clancy, has already been in touch with your superiors. We're supposed to have clearance."

"Wait right here." The officer left, walking over to a man and a woman, both wearing suits, badges hanging from their belts. Words were exchanged and the two suits, obviously detectives, eyed them for a moment then one gave a single nod. The officer beckoned them and the tape was lifted by another. Dawson and Niner joined them.

"I'm Detective Mark Samuel, this is my partner Detective Ella Black. Which one of you is the fiancé?"

"I am," said Dawson. "Can I see her?"

Samuel regarded him. "Her?"

Dawson gestured toward the gurney with the body. "I want to see her before you take her away."

Black glanced over her shoulder at the body bag. "That's not your fiancée, Sergeant."

Niner leaned in. "Sergeant Major."

Black bowed slightly. "Apologies, Sergeant Major. That's a man we've yet to identify."

Dawson exchanged an excited glance with Niner. "You mean she's not dead?"

Samuel shook his head. "I can't say whether she is or isn't. All I can say is that when we arrived on scene, that poor bastard was the only person we found."

Dawson's head swam for a moment and he leaned over, placing his hands on his knees as he drew several breaths, Niner asking the questions now.

"When the other women left, they said they thought they saw her getting shot, but they couldn't be certain." He regarded the dozens of numbered yellow markers laid out on the pavement, shell casings and blood spatter beside each, including a large pool of blood at the entrance of an alleyway. He pointed. "I assume the victim was shot there?"

Black nodded. "He took a couple of rounds to the back then one to the head to finish him off. We believe there were two perpetrators. They then opened fire on the SUV belonging to one Maggie Harris"— she checked her notes— "driven by Vanessa Moore. From what we can gather, she managed to drive them out of here with one Shirley Belme, uninjured, and one Joanne Lightman, deceased."

Niner's jaw dropped as Dawson stood straight. "She's dead?"

"Yes, Sergeant Major, I'm afraid she didn't make it to the hospital."

Dawson gripped his temples as his eyes burned. Niner leaned against him, pressing his head into Dawson's shoulder, and they embraced each other briefly as they mourned their friend's wife. Dawson patted Niner on the back. "Message Red. Let them know about Joanne. Tell them when the debrief is over to go to the hospital. Spock is going to need them."

Niner wiped his eyes dry with his knuckles then walked away, fishing his phone out of his pocket as Dawson regained control. "Is there any evidence that anyone else was shot here?"

"There's blood spatter near where we think the SUV was parked. We're assuming it belongs to the deceased, Joanne Lightman."

"But nothing else?"

"No."

"And there's no sign of my fiancée?"

"No. We've got officers searching the area in case she's injured, but from what was described from the statements given by Vanessa Moore and Shirley Belme, I can't see how she would have escaped. One of the gunmen was apparently straddling her the last time they saw her."

Dawson's fists clenched, his nails biting into his palms as rage built once again. "Could they have let her go?"

"If they did, enough time has passed that she would have reached out to somebody, wouldn't she?"

"Unless they took her phone."

Black shook her head, waving an arm at the road, dozens of businesses and restaurants within sight. "All she'd have to do is go into one of these establishments and ask to use a phone. There's no way we wouldn't have heard from her if they let her go."

"So, what are you saying?"

Samuel frowned. "We believe they took her."

Dawson's stomach dropped and his mouth filled with bile at the thought. He swallowed. "Why would they take her?"

"She's a witness."

"Then why wouldn't they have just killed her?"

"They probably want the other three that got away."

Dawson cursed. "Which means they're not safe."

"We've got officers at the hospital." Black's phone rang and she stepped away as Dawson struggled to not shut down, his racing mind picturing unspeakable things being done to his beloved Maggie. Black joined them a moment later. "We've got an ID on our victim over there." She jerked a thumb toward the gurney. "His name is Sergey Shoygu. He's got quite the record. Member of the Russian mob. Word is he had a falling out with the boss and has been on the run for several months."

"Looks like they finally caught up to him," said Samuel.

"The Russian mob?" Dawson stared at them. "What the hell's the Russian mob doing in Fayetteville?"

Black scanned the file on her phone. "He was based in New York City. They probably just caught up to him here. "

Dawson pulled at his hair. "Okay. They took Maggie. Where would they take her if this isn't where they normally operate?"

Samuel chewed his cheek for a moment. "They probably have a room at some cheap motel where nobody asks questions, but who knows if that's where they'll take her. My guess is they have a vehicle, they put her in it, they're questioning her now or have already questioned her, and they'll arrange for hits on the two surviving women."

Dawson tensed. "As soon as they've finished questioning her, then they have no more use for her."

"Possibly, though they may hold on to her until they've eliminated the other two, just in case. She might have more information that could help them. I think as long as her two friends are alive, she's alive."

Dawson spun on his heel, heading back toward his car.

"Just where do you think you're going?" asked Samuel.

"To make sure that Vanessa and Shirley stay alive."

"I've already got a team watching them. The last thing they need is amateurs getting involved."

Dawson grunted. "We are *not* amateurs." He fired a text to Red.

Russian mob might try to hit Vanessa and Shirley at the hospital. Join us ASAP. Bring supplies.

This wasn't over, not by a long shot. Maggie was out there somewhere, and he had to find her, but first, he had to secure the others, and that wouldn't be at a public hospital. He and his team had to get them to safety, and the best place for that was the Unit.

There was no way the Russian mob would dare attempt a hit on Bragg.

The Unit

Fort Bragg, North Carolina

Red's eyes shot wide at the text message from Dawson, and Colonel Clancy noticed. "What now?"

"BD says the Russian mob might hit the hospital in an attempt to take out Vanessa and Shirley."

Clancy's eyes narrowed. "The Russian mob?"

"Yes, sir. He says to join him there ASAP. With supplies."

Clancy cursed. "Okay, you all can't go, otherwise you'll scare the living shit out of every civilian at that hospital. Sergeant, take three men with you, any non-lethal equipment you want from here, and your personal licensed weapons. No military firepower. Get there, secure the scene, then evac our people back to the Unit. I'll deal with whatever blowback there is. Just secure our family."

Red rose. "Yes, sir." He pointed at Sergeants Trip "Mickey" McDonald, Eugene "Jagger" Thomas, and Zack "Wings" Hauser, and they all followed him out of the room as the rest of the team stayed behind to finish the debriefing.

Niner had updated him a few minutes ago with the fact that Maggie hadn't been found at the scene, and that Spock's wife was dead. There was still hope for Maggie if they acted quickly, but right now, the mission was to secure those they could, and without any intel that might lead to Maggie's location, roaming around town with their heads poking out the windows was a waste of everyone's time and talent.

This had to be treated like an op.

Clancy had activated an ops center, but Red was fully aware they had strict limitations on what they could do, especially on American soil, and it gave him an idea. He sent a message to Dawson.

Recommend we bring Dylan in on this.

The reply was immediate. A thumbs-up.

They entered the supply room and the corporal behind the desk sprang to his feet.

"How can I help you, Sergeant?"

"Make a list. I'm going to say this only once, and I don't want anything missed. I'll need ten of everything." He rapidly rhymed off the pieces of equipment he thought they would need, the others chiming in with their own ideas. The corporal's eyes bulged, looking up from the clipboard he had made his notes on.

"I'm going to need approval for this."

"Colonel Clancy's already approved it. He's in Conference Room Charlie. Open the gate. We'll start getting what we need while you're on the phone. We don't have a second to waste."

"Yes, Sergeant," replied the corporal as he grabbed the phone and buzzed them inside.

They immediately set to work, gathering everything they would need, and as Red donned his body armor, tightening up the straps, he was forced to wonder just how far this would go. Right now, they were setting out to secure his wife and Atlas' girlfriend, but once accomplished, they had to recover Maggie, and that could mean going to war with the Russian mob.

Something he personally had no problem with.

Bring it on.

Cape Fear Valley Medical Center, Fourth Floor

Fayetteville, North Carolina

"ETA?"

"Fifteen minutes," replied Red. "BD and Niner should be there in about five."

Atlas cursed. "I'm not armed, and I don't think Spock is either. We checked our personal weapons at the Unit."

"We've got them. I suggest you move everyone into as secure a room as you can. Once we get there, we've got body armor for everyone. The colonel's authorized us to exfil everyone to the Unit until we can figure out what's going on."

"Copy that. We're sure it's the Russian mob?"

"No, but I talked to BD and he said the victim was former Russian mob who had a falling out with his masters. The locals seem to think they finally caught up to him, and that they took Maggie so they could track down any witnesses to his killing. You know how these guys work. They're brutal."

24

"You're not lying. Get here as soon as you can. I'm going to secure the others."

"Good luck."

Atlas ended the call then walked over to the detectives, introductions having been made earlier. "We need a secure room."

One of the detectives, Clint Sneider, regarded him. "Why?"

"Apparently, the Russian mob is involved, and we have reason to believe they might attempt to eliminate the surviving witnesses."

Sneider's partner, Veronica Lance, eyed him. "Who's we?"

"My associates."

"And what makes you think the Russian mob's involved?" Sneider's tone dripped with disrespect.

Atlas' fists clenched. "Do you people not talk to each other? The victim at the shooting has been identified as former Russian mob, on the outs with those he used to work for. They believe this was a hit and that Maggie was taken so that they could track down the other witnesses. This is the Russian mob. They don't play by the same rules you're used to."

"Oh? And just what rules are we used to?"

Atlas drew a deep breath and held up a hand. "Listen, I'm not trying to offend you, but this is what I do for a living. All I'm asking for is a secure room and more officers. The last thing we want is a shootout in a hospital."

"There's not going to be any shootout. There's no way anyone's going to risk a hit here, it's too public."

Atlas sighed. "You don't know these people. I deal with these types all the time. They don't act like the typical gangs you're used to here. These aren't small-time, common street thugs. The Russian mob is different. They are completely loyal. They will do anything that's asked of them by those above them in the chain of command. No hesitation. No concerns about dying. Think Yakuza, not Bloods and Crips. If they're ordered to hit this hospital and eliminate the witnesses, they will do it even if they know they're going to die. But they're also not stupid. They'll try to infiltrate, not just do a full-frontal assault. Every minute we talk here is a minute wasted that could be spent preparing for what might be coming. I'm not saying they *will* attack, I'm saying they could. We need to prepare for that possibility."

Sneider frowned. "You're military, aren't you?"

"Yes."

"Army?"

"Yes."

"I assume you served in Afghanistan and Iraq."

"Where I served is irrelevant."

"Oh, I think it's very relevant. You see threats everywhere you look and you overreact. We're not in a warzone. This is Fayetteville. Gunmen aren't hiding around every corner."

Atlas cursed. "What is your malfunction? Why are you ignoring the obvious? Is it because I'm military? Do you have something against people who serve your country?"

Sneider jabbed a finger at him. "I serve my country too. Day in, day out, I protect the streets. I solve the crimes that affect people here in America, not in some foreign country, yet I'm spit on and called corrupt, and called a racist, just because of the job I do. You guys go overseas and fight in bullshit wars that accomplish nothing, and you're the heroes. You don't hear anybody screaming, 'Defund the military,' or to completely dismantle it. What would happen to

America if all the police went home tomorrow? It would be open season on innocent civilians. You guys get all the money and all the glory, and we get accused of being horrible people when we're arresting scum who have committed crimes or are deliberately defying our lawful orders. So yeah, forgive me if I don't listen to somebody who has no experience being a police officer, and no experience in these matters. If we were in Iraq, you would ignore my advice, just like I'm ignoring yours. Nobody's going to attack a hospital. I think it's best you go home before I charge you with interfering in an investigation."

Atlas growled, his muscles bulging. "You arrogant bastard! You're taking your hatred of the military and your anger over a protest movement, and are putting innocent lives at risk."

Lance repositioned between Sneider and Atlas. "Just everybody calm down. We'll take them into protective custody."

Atlas glared at Sneider then turned his attention to the more reasonable Lance. "Talk some sense into your partner. I don't give a shit what he says or tries to do, I'm going to protect our people even if you won't. If you're not going to help, then stay the hell out of my way." He turned on his heel and walked over to the nurse's station. "I need a room, preferably with no outside windows, with a door that can lock from the inside."

The nurse, who had apparently overheard the exchange, pointed down the hall. "Room 408. The residents use it for sleeping. I don't know if anyone's in it now, though."

"Thank you."

The nurse leaned forward. "Thank you for your service."

Atlas flashed her a grateful smile then jogged down the hallway to the room in question. He opened the door and found a small room with a pair of bunkbeds, none occupied. It had no windows, and only the one door. It would have to do. He rejoined the others, huddled outside of the ICU.

Vanessa hugged him. "What's going on? I thought you were about to give that detective a beat-down."

"He came within an inch of it, let me tell you." He lowered his voice. "Listen, we think the Russian mob's involved and that they took Maggie so that they could find you, Shirley, and Joanne."

"Find us? Why?" asked Shirley.

"You're witnesses."

Her face paled. "You mean…"

Vanessa finished her thought. "You mean they want to kill us?"

"Possibly. The police aren't taking it seriously, or at least that one asshole isn't. I want the two of you in that room." He pointed in the direction of 408. "Go inside and lock the door and don't open it unless you hear one of our voices or the coded knock. Three knocks followed by one then two. Got it?"

"Three, one, two. Yes."

"Okay, now go."

Vanessa took Shirley by the hand and they rushed down the hallway, disappearing inside the room, Atlas watching the entire time. He sucked in a long breath then knocked on the ICU door before opening it. Spock sat on the edge of Joanne's bed, one hand holding his dead wife's to his chest while the other gently stroked her hair.

"I think we've got a problem. I need your help."

Spock sniffed, and with his head still turned away from Atlas, he wiped the tears from his face. "What's going on?"

"They identified the victim at the shooting scene as Russian mob, apparently someone that betrayed them, and police think it was a hit. Maggie's missing and the going theory is that she was taken so they could find Vanessa and Shirley. BD and Niner are on their way, and Red's on his way with some of the guys and our personal weapons. We have to secure our people until the others arrive, then we're going to extract them to the Unit. I could really use your help."

Spock nodded, still clasping his wife's hand to his chest. "I don't have my weapon."

"Neither do I."

Spock rose and faced Atlas, his eyes red, his cheeks stained. "Just let me get my hands on them. I don't need a gun."

Atlas smiled slightly then flexed his arms. "I always bring these guns with me wherever I go."

Spock laughed then headed for the door. "We're going to need a secure room."

Atlas led them out. "Already done. Now, let's just hope the guys get here before the Russians."

Cape Fear Valley Medical Center Parking Garage

Fayetteville, North Carolina

Grigori twisted the man's neck, the satisfying snap something he would never tire of. Guns were too impersonal. He preferred his hands. He wanted to feel the warmth of his victim's body, he wanted to hear their last breath, he wanted to smell their fear. Shooting someone from a distance with a gun deprived him of all that. It took the joy out of killing. It didn't mean he was averse to using one—it simply meant for close quarters, he preferred the personal touch.

He propped the doctor against the rear of the luxury SUV his victim had arrived in and pulled off the man's lab coat. He donned it then resecured the ID that had dropped off during the brief struggle. He fished the fob out of the man's pocket then popped the rear hatch, dumping the body inside and closing it before striding quickly out of the parking garage beside the hospital, and toward the entrance to the main building and its bank of elevators.

He was the first to arrive on the scene. He had three targets all identified by their prisoner, Maggie Harris. She had refused to give them any information at first, but a dozen blows to the face, chest, and stomach, then a promise to cut her breasts off, had her talking. The boss was heading back to New York shortly and the hit team standing by at a motel just outside of the city were on their way, though he suspected the targets would be eliminated before they arrived.

By him.

The elevator doors opened and he held out a hand, smiling as two women boarded before him. He stepped on, and one of them asked, "Which floor?"

"Fourth, please."

She pressed the button and it lit up, the door sliding closed. This would all be over in the next five minutes. Either he would be dead, or his targets. Either way, he didn't care. He never expected to survive a job—he always went in thinking he was already dead. It gave him a certain sense of freedom. He would be facing police officers at most, and from his experience, they were easy to deal with, especially when you were committed. A police officer would hesitate to draw his weapon as you charged toward him, especially these days when everyone was concerned with being accused of something, and those precious seconds lost were all he usually needed to be on top of them, a knife silently plunging into their neck.

The doors opened to the fourth floor and he stepped off. He checked left then right, his expert eyes taking in everything. The nurse's station was just ahead to his left, a uniformed officer stood near an ICU door, and two detectives huddled nearby, one talking to someone on the phone, the other tapping away at hers. To his right, there were no obvious police, but one man stood at the far corner, his stained face suggesting he was in a tremendous amount of grief, and, closer to the elevators, lurked a hulking Black man, his head on a swivel.

They made eye contact briefly, but Grigori ignored him, instead turning left and striding toward the ICU guarded by the police officer. He snapped out a nod to the man who merely glanced to see that he was wearing an ID, not bothering to check the photo. The officer bowed his head slightly and Grigori stepped inside, finding the room empty save a woman lying on the bed, all the monitors turned off. He stepped over and checked for a pulse but didn't bother searching after he touched her—she was ice cold. He took a photo of her face with his phone, one part of his job already done.

"Hey, why are you taking her photo?"

Grigori slipped his phone back in his pocket and turned with a smile to see the police officer standing in the doorway. "Just for the record."

"Bullshit." The officer stepped toward Grigori, his hand extended. "Let me see your ID."

"No problem, officer." Grigori unclipped it from the pocket of his lab coat and handed it over. The officer took it, his eyes narrowing as he realized the pictures didn't match.

"Hey, wait a minute."

It was the last thing the man would ever say. Grigori's hand darted out and gripped the man's throat, his fingers digging in. If the officer had reached for his gun, he might have stood a chance, however remote, but instead, he instinctually used both of his hands to grab at Grigori's, and that split-second error in judgment would spell the man's doom. Grigori hauled him closer, spinning him around, then released the grip, grabbing the man by the face and the rear of the skull, twisting hard.

Another snap.

Two in one day was rare. He inhaled deeply, smelling the man's shampoo, his cheap cologne, his terror.

Intoxicating.

Grigori dragged him behind the bed and dropped him unceremoniously on the floor. He took the man's radio and turned it off, placing it in an inner pocket in case he might need to monitor police communications later. He took the officer's badge and tucked it into another pocket, then headed out of the room and turned to his left, walking past the detectives who hadn't yet noticed the officer was missing. He strode toward the far end of the hall and turned right down another corridor, breathing a little easier now that he was out of sight.

The grieving man and the Black man had to be involved somehow. They weren't police, so who were they? Fort Bragg was close by. Could they be military? If so, then the tactics he normally used wouldn't necessarily work on them. Combat veterans wouldn't hesitate. They drew their weapon and shot, then asked questions later. And depending on who they were, they could be trained to counter any move he might make, including what he had already used successfully twice in the past five minutes.

Their presence changed everything.

The question was, where were the other two women that he was after? The answer likely lay between where the two men were positioned. There were at least half a dozen doors between the men down that corridor. The doors on the side of the elevator would be on the outside of the building, meaning windows, and vulnerable to snipers. If these men were experienced, they would put them in an inner room. He turned right and walked along another corridor, heading for the far end, the rooms there opposite those he suspected his targets were hiding in.

He found three doors and chose the one in the middle, finding it unlocked. He stepped inside then closed the door behind him, pressing the button on the knob to lock it. He was in a janitor's closet. It was cramped, but there should be little chance of discovery. There was a utility sink in the corner and he turned the tap on, creating white noise to muffle any sounds he might make. He stepped over to the far wall and grabbed a small step ladder. He opened it then climbed the few steps to the acoustic tiles overhead. He slid one aside then poked his head through. He was surrounded by an array of tiles, wires, and cobwebs, along with pipes and conduits crisscrossing the anonymous rooms. The elevator shafts were to the right, columns supporting the structure spaced out all around him.

He cocked an ear and listened. Two women were talking nearby, the only voices he could hear with little difficulty. It had to be his targets, and they had to be close. He pulled himself up, propping himself atop the cinderblock wall. He reached out with both hands, bracing himself, then leaned forward, tilting his head so his ear was parallel to the acoustic tile on the other side.

"How much longer do you think?"

"I don't know. I didn't notice what time it was when we came in here, but it has to have been at least five minutes, hasn't it?"

"No idea. I haven't been able to think straight. I can't believe Joanne is dead. I feel so bad for Spock."

Grigori smiled. It was them. It was his two remaining targets. As much as he'd like to drop into the room and kill them both with his bare hands, this wasn't the time for that. The two men he had spotted were obviously guarding the women, and he couldn't risk his targets making any sounds that might tip their protectors off.

He drew his weapon from his shoulder holster then carefully screwed the suppressor in place. All he had to do now was pry aside another acoustic tile, fire two shots, then two more to confirm the kills, then extract himself without anyone knowing he had ever been there. Security footage would be checked, of course, and he would be seen on camera, but that didn't concern him. The authorities knew who he was—they could just never get their hands on him.

He repositioned, his weapon pressed between the cinderblock and his hand. He leaned forward and pried open an acoustic tile directly in front of him. He lifted it several inches, then leaned closer, peering inside. Two women sat below him on a cot, the top bunkbed shielding him from view, only their knees, shoulders, and, critically, their heads, visible as they stared at the floor.

This would be easier than he thought.

He lifted the tile up several more inches, hooking it on a dangling wire, freeing up his left hand. He repositioned, shifting his weight to the left, freeing up his right hand with his suppressed weapon. This was it. The contract was about to be fulfilled. He slowly guided his weapon from its resting place on the cinderblock and carefully took aim, his finger transferring to the trigger from the guard.

He smiled.

I love my job.

He loved the thrill of the kill, and he loved the massive bonus he would get from the boss for cleaning up these loose ends.

There was a crash behind him and he nearly lost his balance as he twisted around. He spotted the locked door swinging open, the top hinge torn from the frame. An impossibly deep growl echoed through the confined space then he suddenly felt iron grips on both of his ankles before he was pulled unceremoniously from his perch. His chin slammed onto the cinderblock as he was dragged backward. He squeezed the trigger as he redirected the weapon back into the other room, repeatedly firing as screams erupted on the other side of the wall. He continued to be hauled back into the janitor's closet and he collapsed onto the step ladder, several ribs cracking or breaking.

The grip on his right ankle released and as he tried to kick out, his right hand was grabbed with a force so strong, he was convinced whatever was attacking him couldn't possibly be human. The hold on his left ankle was released, and a second hand joined the first, grabbing his right forearm as the rest of his body collapsed across the ladder. His right arm was picked up then shoved down rapidly, and he could feel the bones in his forearm snap in half. He cried out in agony as the gun clattered to the ground.

He collapsed to the floor and onto his back, finally giving him a view of his assailant. It was the massive Black man he had made brief eye contact with. Grigori's body was in excruciating pain, but the fight wasn't out of him. He had experienced pain before. He was former Spetsnaz, Russia's elite Special Forces. He had committed unspeakable acts on behalf of his government, and had unspeakable things done to him. With his left hand, he reached down and pulled a knife from his belt, then swung. The arc was interrupted with a block, then a flurry of blows to his face. The block slammed his hand against the cold concrete of the floor, then a boot crushed his wrist, the knife clattering onto the hard surface.

This fight was over.

He wasn't going to win.

It had been a good run. He had had a good life and he had no regrets. He reached back with his tongue and closed his eyes, biting down on the plastic capsule he always tucked in his cheek while on the job. He felt the cyanide pill's effects immediately. His body jerked, his mouth foaming as the poison did its job far slower than he had been told it would take, but it didn't matter. The pain from the pill was nothing compared to the broken bones, and as he shook, the massive man stepped back, cursing.

"Who sent you? Give me a name!"

Grigori desperately wanted to flip the man off, but his hands weren't working anymore. He opened his mouth to spit one final insult but managed only a gurgle as the room fell dark and he readied for what was to come, either nothing, for the afterlife was a lie told to the sheep to keep them in line, or an eternity in Hell, for he refused to believe any god could possibly forgive him for the sins he had committed during his limited days on this Earth.

Atlas shook his head as the death rattle finished, then he righted the ladder and climbed up, poking his head over the edge. "Are you two okay?" he shouted before he could see Vanessa and Shirley.

"Vanessa's been shot!" cried Shirley.

Atlas rolled over the cinderblock and fell onto the top bunk. He swung his legs over and onto the floor then unlocked the door and yanked it open. "Spock, get in here!" He turned his attention to Vanessa, lying on the bottom cot, gripping her shoulder. "Were you hit in the shoulder?"

"Yeah."

"She saved my life!" cried Shirley. "She threw herself over me as the shots were fired all around us!"

Spock appeared in the doorway then cursed. "What the hell happened here?"

Atlas jerked a thumb at the far wall he had just cleared. "Hitman in the other room. He's dead, probably a cyanide capsule. Get over there and get any weapons he has. He's not going to be alone."

Spock jumped, grabbing the top of the wall under the propped open acoustic tile, then disappeared onto the other side, reappearing a few moments later with the man's weapons.

Atlas gently moved Vanessa's hand and was relieved to see the bullet had gone all the way through her upper arm. He grabbed the pillow from the bed and tore the pillowcase off, then tied a tourniquet just above the wound. "You're going to be okay. It's a through-and-through."

"What are we going to do?" asked Shirley.

"She needs a doctor but it can wait," replied Atlas. He pulled out his phone and sent a text message.

ETA?

2 minutes.

We're in room 408. Just foiled a hit. They know we're here and where we are.

Understood. We're pulling in now. Be ready to go in 60 seconds.

Atlas shoved his phone back in his pocket. "They're here. We're going to get you two to the Unit where you'll be safe."

Vanessa, tears in her eyes, looked up at him from the cot. "Then what? Are we supposed to go through life in constant fear, waiting for the next hitman?"

Spock interrupted Atlas' reply. "The only people who should be afraid now are the bastards behind this. I want every one of them dead."

Vanessa grimaced as she stood. "So do I."

Cape Fear Valley Medical Center, Main Entrance

Fayetteville, North Carolina

Wings pulled up to the hospital's main entrance in a Humvee, borrowed unceremoniously, approval requested and received from Clancy as they rolled toward the gate with the MPs preparing to block them. They had blasted out of Bragg with Jagger's pickup truck on their bumper, in their haste breaking too many traffic laws to count. Red was on the ground before they came to a halt, heading for the door as he pointed at Wings. "Watch the vehicles and keep an eye out for any suspicious arrivals."

"Roger that."

Mickey and Jagger grabbed large duffel bags from the back and followed. Shocked civilians parted like the Red Sea as an armed Moses headed for the elevators. The doors opened and the crowd waiting to get on board scurried out of the way as the three men in full body armor boarded. Red punched the button for the fourth floor as an alarm sounded, security rushing toward them as the doors closed.

"Well, somebody thinks we're terrorists," said Mickey.

Red drew his weapon. "I just hope nobody gets any stupid ideas and tries to play hero." The door chimed as it opened and Red stepped out, breaking left as Jagger handed his bag to Mickey then followed, breaking right. Red scanned the area. "Clear!" Jagger echoed him and Mickey stepped out, holding the door with his foot.

"Where's 408?" shouted Red at the nurse's station.

A shaky finger pointed to their right.

"What the hell's going on here?"

Red glanced at a police detective he had already noticed. "I'm Master Sergeant Belme. We're here to secure our people. I recommend you stand aside." Red then ignored the detective and his partner and broke right. He found 408 and knocked on the door. "Atlas, Spock, it's Red."

The door opened and Mickey tossed the duffel bags into the corridor, still holding the elevator door. Jagger grabbed them then threw them into the room.

"Gear up," said Red. "There's body armor for everyone, and your personal weapons." He noticed Vanessa's arm. "Is she good to get to Bragg?" he asked as Atlas unzipped the bags and handed out gear.

"Through-and-through. She'll be fine. We'll patch her up en route." Atlas' eyes narrowed as he donned his body armor. "Wait a minute. How the hell did you two get here before BD and Niner?"

Across from Cape Fear Valley Medical Center

Fayetteville, North Carolina

The moment Dawson heard Vanessa and Shirley were secure in a locked room, he had changed the plan. Rather than rendezvous with Atlas and Spock at the hospital, he had decided covering their egress was more critical. Instead, he and Niner had taken the high ground across from the hospital entrance. From the rooftop of a three-story commercial building and through the scope of his AR-15 that he kept locked in the trunk of his Mustang, they watched as more of the team arrived, Wings remaining outside to guard the vehicles. In his concern for Maggie, he had forgotten about the semi-automatic weapon until Niner reminded him on their way to the hospital, triggering the development of a new plan.

He couldn't walk into a hospital with an AR-15 on full display, but he could cover its entrance from the roof of the building across the street. If the Russians were indeed coming, his people could be sitting ducks because he had no doubt the six Glocks on the ground would be no match for the firepower the Russians would bring. If his guys were properly equipped with MP5s or M4s, they could hold their own in any fight, but those were military weapons that they didn't have access to.

His lone AR-15 would have to do the job.

He dialed Red's number and put the phone on speaker, sitting it between him and Niner, acting as his spotter.

"BD, where the hell are you two?"

"Across the street in an overseer position. I've got my AR-15."

"Understood. Any sign of hostile activity?"

"Negative. What's your situation?"

"Vanessa has a through-and-through in her upper right arm. Other than that, we're good. We're gearing up now. Should be outside in under two minutes."

"Copy that. Put your phone on speaker and leave the line open."

"Roger that. Is everybody ready?"

A round of affirmatives were heard through the speaker.

"Beginning extraction now."

"Copy that," said Dawson. "Good luck."

Cape Fear Valley Medical Center, Fourth Floor

Fayetteville, North Carolina

Red opened the door, poking his head out, checking left and right. "Are we clear?" he called to Jagger, still holding the elevator, its alarm protesting loudly.

"Affirmative."

"Then let's go." Red stepped out, immediately followed by Mickey, covering them on the left as Atlas and Spock each guided one of their charges toward the elevator. Red joined Jagger, covering right as they advanced.

"Where the hell do you think you're taking them?" It was the male detective.

"We're taking them to Bragg. Contact Colonel Clancy. He's coordinating this with your superiors."

"Bullshit!" The man stormed toward them, his partner on his heels. "You have no authority here. I can't count how many laws you've broken already."

Atlas helped Vanessa onto the elevator then Spock did the same with Shirley as Red backed in, his weapon at the ready. "I'd love to talk, Detective, but check the opposite room. There's a body of a hitman in there, which just proves your security is bullshit. We're going to protect our people. You can charge me with whatever you want. This is self-defense and our weapons are licensed and we're acting as private citizens."

Mickey cleared the door and Jagger removed his foot, the protesting doors slowly closing. The detective rushed forward, jamming a hand between the doors, then boarded with them along with his partner.

"If you're going to take my only two damned witnesses, I'm going with you."

The doors shut as Red pushed the two detectives to the side, he and Mickey taking up position at the front. "You can come with us, but just remember one thing."

"What's that?"

"We shoot to kill."

Across from Cape Fear Valley Medical Center

Fayetteville, North Carolina

Dawson slowly scanned the crowd as scores of people surged out the entrance as the alarm continued to sound.

"This could pose a problem," commented Niner as he peered through a pair of binoculars also kept in Dawson's trunk.

Dawson had to agree. If this turned into a gunfight, a lot of innocent people could die. If the Russian mob were indeed sending a team in, he had to head them off before they reached the entrance. There had been no time for details, but the fact Vanessa was wounded meant the Russians had already made an attempt, and it reaffirmed that his decision to get their people to safety on the base had been the right one.

"Nine o'clock."

Dawson swung his scope toward the target.

"Black SUV heading toward us, weaving in and out of traffic."

Dawson cursed. "Red. Status?"

"Coming out of the main floor elevators now."

"We might have company. Get a move on."

"Roger that."

Dawson squinted slightly as he got a bead on the driver. He adjusted left and caught a glimpse of the passenger, a submachine gun gripped against his chest. There was no doubt now. "This is them. Passenger is armed with an HK."

Niner cursed. "I'm counting four in the vehicle."

Dawson adjusted his scope, checking the main entrance, his team nowhere in sight. "Red, what's your status?"

"Stand by. We've walked into a Charlie-Foxtrot."

Cape Fear Valley Medical Center, Main Floor
Fayetteville, North Carolina

Red kept his weapon aimed at the floor as half a dozen police officers aimed their own directly at him and his team.

"Drop your weapons!" ordered one of the men as Red advanced slowly out of the elevator.

"I have no intention of doing that, officer. These are licensed weapons. We are evacuating our people to safety. There's already been an assassination attempt on the fourth floor. I suggest you secure this building. The threat is outside and approaching."

"ETA sixty seconds," said Dawson over the speaker.

Red continued to slowly step out of the elevator, the others following. He looked over his shoulder at the male detective. "This is when you choose sides."

The man appeared hesitant, uncertain as to what to do, but he remained silent, instead glancing at his partner, who appeared equally uncertain.

"We don't have time for this." Red pointed toward the exit. "We're going out that door, getting in our vehicles, and heading to Bragg. Call our commanding officer, Colonel Thomas Clancy. We'll straighten out everything once we have our people safe." Red headed for the door when the officer screamed at him.

"Drop your weapon and raise your hands or we'll shoot!"

Atlas, Spock, Mickey, and Jagger raised their weapons, pointing them directly at the officers they were squared off against. Red kept his aimed at the floor as he calmly turned then took two steps toward the officer. "Have you ever killed a man?"

The officer's gun was aimed directly at Red's chest. "What?"

"I said, have you ever killed a man?"

"No."

Red tilted his head toward the others on his team. "We've killed at least a dozen in the past week. You won't survive this. We're not the bad guys here, and you know it. Stand down and this becomes a paperwork exercise. Engage us, and you will lose." He turned to the detective. "For the love of God, make a decision!"

The man stood wide-eyed then finally the woman squared her jaw and stepped out of the elevator. "Everybody stand down. He's right. We're all on the same side here."

Dawson's voice came over the phone tucked in Red's pocket, everyone turning toward him.

"The Russians have arrived. Engaging now."

Red turned. "Let's get the hell out of here."

And as he sprinted toward the door, gunfire from an AR-15 opened up outside.

Across from Cape Fear Valley Medical Center

Fayetteville, North Carolina

The SUV turned onto the hospital grounds and Dawson made the call. He couldn't allow them to gain access to the hospital, or the throng in front of it. "Engaging now." He took aim at the engine compartment, squeezing the trigger repeatedly, the semi-automatic weapon belching lead. For now, his task wasn't to take out those inside—it was to stop their means of pursuit.

The vehicle swerved as the driver realized what was happening and took evasive action, but Dawson's position gave him the advantage and he continued to fire, emptying an entire mag into the engine as the SUV shuddered to a halt, steam erupting from under the hood. He ejected the empty mag and reloaded, directing his attention to those inside.

"Vehicle disabled. Engaging occupants," he reported. He put two through the driver's side windshield, then two more through the passenger side as Niner spotted.

"Driver down. Passenger caught one in the shoulder."

Dawson continued to fire as the rear doors flew open, the passengers pouring out and retreating to the back of the vehicle before he had a chance to get a bead on them. One leaned out and opened fire at their position, the fully automatic weapon spraying bullets toward them. Dawson and Niner both rolled back, allowing the building's facade to protect them. "Our position is compromised. Two, possibly three hostiles still engaged," he shouted to Red.

"Copy that. Exiting the building now."

"Copy that," replied Dawson. "You should see a black SUV directly in front of you, less than one hundred yards."

"Copy that, exiting now."

Cape Fear Valley Medical Center, Main Floor

Fayetteville, North Carolina

Red pointed at Mickey and Jagger. "You two with me. We'll provide cover fire if necessary. Atlas and Spock, you get them inside the Humvee. We'll take the truck."

"Roger that," acknowledged Atlas.

Red advanced through the inner doors then paused at the outer, peering at the scene outside. Wings was taking cover on the passenger side of the Humvee, his weapon aimed at the black SUV at the entrance to the hospital grounds. Muzzle flashes indicated their position as they fired on a building across the street, and as long as they did that, they weren't paying attention to what was happening here. "Let's go." He pushed open the door and stepped outside, rushing toward Wings' position. "Friendlies on your six."

Wings didn't bother turning to confirm it. He and Jagger broke left, heading between the two vehicles, aiming their weapons but not engaging as Atlas rushed forward. He yanked open the rear door and Red watched out of the corner of his eye from the front bumper as the big man helped Vanessa and Shirley in the back before slamming the door shut. Spock entered through the passenger side then climbed into the driver's seat, firing up the engine as Atlas joined him.

Red pointed directly ahead along the front of the building. "Ambulance exit is that way. Follow it. It should take you away from the hostiles. Just get to the base. Don't stop for anyone."

"Roger that." Spock put the vehicle in gear and pulled away.

"Let's go." Red extended his weapon in front of him as he advanced toward the enemy. He lowered his chin, bringing it closer to his phone tucked in a vest pocket. "BD, do you copy?"

"We copy."

"We're advancing on their position now. You should have some relief in fifteen seconds."

"Copy that. Preparing to reengage."

The four of them spread out so as not to provide a clumped target, and continued their rapid but controlled advance. A police car wailed down the road toward the hospital, its lights flashing, and gunfire was redirected at the vehicle, the automatic weapons making quick work of it, sending the unit careening out of control before it came to a violent halt, slamming into the side of a building.

Red prayed whoever was inside was still alive, but thanked them for the distraction. "Prepare to engage." He took aim at the man who had just blown away the squad car. "Engage."

All four weapons opened fire, and a moment later Dawson's AR-15 joined from the roof across the street. Within seconds it was over, the Russians down. Red and the others continued to advance, not letting down their guard lest someone was only down and not out. They reached their targets and Red frowned, a little disappointed to find them all dead.

There was no one to interrogate.

He turned to Jagger. "Get photos of them all."

"Yes, Sergeant."

Jagger snapped shots of the dead that they could use to identify them later against their databases, and hopefully Vanessa and Shirley would be able to confirm if any of them had been involved in the attack that had led to Joanne's death and Maggie's kidnapping. Police officers swarmed the area, as well as the two detectives. Red holstered his weapon as did the others. He handed the detective a card.

"We'll be leaving now. Call the base to arrange a time to come in for any questions you might have."

The man's mouth was agape, his eyes wide, his hand slowly shaking the card. "I've never seen anything like that! That was incredible!"

Shouts erupted from several officers as they aimed their weapons toward the building across the street, Dawson emerging with an AR-15 slung over his shoulder with Niner beside him.

"They're with us!" said Red, and the detective shouted for everyone to lower their weapons. Dawson and Niner joined them a moment later.

Dawson's experienced eye surveyed the scene. "Report."

"Atlas and Spock have taken Vanessa and Shirley to the Unit. They should be there in ten minutes. Unless there's a reason to stick around, we should head out too."

Dawson's eyes scanned the crowd and they settled on the detective. "Are you in charge?"

"I'm Detective Sneider. This is my partner Detective Lance. This is our scene. Who the hell are you?"

Dawson ignored the question. "Who's the lead detective on the case?"

"We're assisting Detectives Samuel and Black. Samuel is the lead."

"Good, I've met them." Dawson removed a card from his pocket and wrote down a number. He handed it to the detective. "This is my personal cell number. Have Detective Samuel call me as soon as possible." He indicated the chaos around them. "As you can see, we can be of assistance, even if it's unofficial. The missing woman is Maggie Harris and she's my fiancée. We should coordinate our efforts to find her."

Sneider tucked the card in his shirt pocket. "While I appreciate your assistance here, this is a civilian matter. Let us do our job. We'll find her and we'll bring her home."

Dawson frowned. "You don't know who you're up against. Look what just went down here. If my men hadn't been here, it would have been a bloodbath."

Sneider scoffed at Dawson and pointed at the dead bodies. "They didn't even make it past the entrance. My men would have stopped them."

Jagger, finished with his photos, tore aside the half-open shirt of the driver, revealing full-body tattoos, then shoved the man's shirt sleeve up, yanking the arm out of the window. "BD, check this out."

Dawson turned and eyed the tattoo, pointing at it then eyeballing the detective. "Do you know what that is?"

Sneider shook his head. "I haven't a clue. If it's some gang tatt, who cares? Like I said, we'll deal with them."

"That's a Spetsnaz tattoo. Russian Special Forces. That means these guys are elite troops, trained for this type of assault. The only reason any of you or your men are alive is because we were here and they didn't realize they were walking into a trap. You don't know what you've got yourself involved in, Detective.

You *will* want our help, or a lot of innocent people will die." Dawson raised a finger in the air and swirled it. "Let's go." He marched toward the pickup truck, still parked in front of the hospital entrance, the gathered police officers parting as the Delta members marched past.

"Wait a minute! We have to take statements. This is a crime scene. You're involved."

Red smiled slightly as Dawson continued forward. "Contact the base. They'll coordinate everything. Right now, we have to get back to our people and make sure they're secure." Dawson climbed into the passenger seat and Jagger took the wheel. Red and Niner took the rear seat while Mickey and Wings jumped into the bed of the truck, no doubt breaking some traffic law. Dawson pointed ahead. "Take us home. We'll collect the other vehicles once everyone is secure."

"You got it." Jagger gunned them away from the entrance and toward Bragg where Atlas and the others would be arriving any moment. And as Red sat back in his seat and closed his eyes, he had no doubt his best friend was consumed with thoughts of his fiancée and where she was.

And what might be happening to her.

This was far from over.

Fort Bragg, North Carolina

IDs were shown and they were cleared through the front gates of Fort Bragg, everyone relieved as Spock guided them toward the secluded corner that housed the Unit. Bragg was home to over 50,000 active-duty personnel, only a portion of which were Delta. It was the worst kept secret next to Area 51. They weren't officially there, but everyone knew they were, and as they pulled into the parking lot near the Unit, Atlas scanned the area. It was late now, most people gone home. He trusted everyone here, but anything was possible. Someone could have infiltrated the base, or there could be a sniper.

Anything.

Shirley helped Vanessa toward the door of the building as Atlas and Spock covered them, and it wasn't until they were inside with the door closed that Atlas breathed easy.

"We need a medic!" shouted Spock, and several heads poked out of doors. A moment later a combat medic rushed down the hallway with a medkit. They stepped into a conference room and the woman went to work on Vanessa's arm.

"Is she going to be okay?" asked Atlas, finally allowing himself to be concerned for his girlfriend.

"She'll be fine," said the medic. "It's a through-and-through. It just needs to be cleaned up. A shot of antibiotics, some wound care, and she'll be fine." The woman smiled up at Vanessa. "But you're going to have a cool scar to show people at parties."

Vanessa winced as the medic irrigated the wound. "I always thought getting shot would hurt more." She gave Atlas a look. "I don't know what you've been complaining about."

Atlas rolled his eyes. "Take one to a thigh or the chest and then get back to me."

The door swung open and Colonel Clancy entered. "Report."

Atlas squared his shoulders, facing his commanding officer. "Sir, we secured our people in an inner room on the fourth floor of the hospital. I spotted a man coming off the elevator who then went into Joanne Lightman's ICU room. A police officer followed him in a few seconds later. The man then left but the police officer didn't return to his post. I observed the man head to the opposite end of the floor, then turn down a corridor that would bring him into an adjacent corridor. I spotted him cross past the opposite side of the nurses' station. I then pursued. I found him inside a room about to open fire on our people. I engaged him, but not before he fired several unaimed rounds. I disarmed him, then attempted an interrogation, however he swallowed some sort of poison that he appeared to already have inside his mouth."

Clancy eyed him. "You mean like a cyanide capsule in the tooth?"

Atlas shrugged. "It seemed like that. I didn't see him put anything in his mouth, so I'm assuming it was already there. I'm sure the autopsy will let us know."

"It would be a first." Clancy dismissed the speculation with a wave of a hand. "Continue."

"I came over the wall into the room Vanessa and Shirley were in, called for Spock, then applied a tourniquet to Vanessa's arm. Red arrived with the others shortly after that. We began our evac, had an altercation with the police in the lobby as we came out of the elevators, but that was defused. From a roof across the street from the hospital, BD and Niner engaged the hostiles arriving in an SUV. We left the building while the hostiles were distracted, and Spock and I evac'd Vanessa and Shirley from the scene then came here. What happened after, I'm not sure."

"That's fine. I'll get the rest from Red." Clancy turned to Vanessa. "How are you feeling, Miss Moore?"

She shrugged then winced, regretting the motion. "As well as can be expected, sir. I just feel so bad for Joanne, and of course you, Spock, and your daughter."

Spock said nothing, instead giving her good shoulder a squeeze before turning away.

Shirley wiped away a tear. "Has there been any word on Maggie?"

Clancy shook his head. "Nothing. We managed to find some footage of her being led into an alleyway by two men. I'm going to the ops center now to see if we've been able to trace her beyond that." He turned to Spock. "I've notified SOS to get you and your family some help, and the chaplain is waiting for you. If there's anything you need, you just ask. I'll make it happen."

Spock stared at the floor. "Thank you, Colonel, but right now I'd like to focus on Maggie."

Clancy clasped Spock's shoulder. "I understand, son, but right now you've got a daughter to think about. Let us worry about Maggie. You worry about your family."

Spock's shoulders slumped. "Yes, sir. You're right, of course."

Clancy gestured at Atlas. "Take him. The chaplain is just down the hall. SOS sent a rep with him that will help coordinate everything. I'll keep you guys posted on Maggie."

"Yes, sir," said Atlas as he and Spock left the room.

Clancy regarded Vanessa as the medic rose. "I've done everything I can do here. She'll have to have the dressing changed tomorrow morning and assigned proper wound care."

"Her prognosis?" asked Clancy.

"Oh, she'll be fine as long as it's looked after properly. She'll make a full recovery."

Vanessa rose and Shirley took her hand, facing Clancy. "How can we help?"

Clancy smiled. "I think you two have been through enough tonight, don't you?"

Shirley shook her head. "Joanne's dead and Maggie is missing." She glanced at Vanessa. "I don't know about you, but there's no way I'm getting any sleep tonight."

Vanessa agreed. "Me neither. There must be something we can do other than just sitting and waiting for a phone call."

Clancy regarded them both. "I'll tell you what. Both of you sit down and get comfortable. I'll have some food and water sent in for you along with something to write with. I want you to both write down every single thing you remember, every detail, no matter how unimportant it may seem, while it's still fresh in your mind, right from the moment you left the shop to the moment you got here. Write it all down."

He turned to Vanessa. "And you, Miss Moore, don't be a hero. You need your rest. The moment you feel tired, I want you to get some shuteye. We've arranged accommodations for you both until this blows over. You need to rest. I know you want to help, but if we're going to bring whoever is responsible to justice, the last thing Atlas and Red need is to be worrying about you two. Let us do our jobs and you do yours by taking care of yourselves."

Vanessa sighed. "You're right, of course, Colonel." She looked at Shirley. "We're just going to get in the way. Let's let the guys do their job and stay out of their hair. The adrenaline we're running on isn't going to last much longer anyway."

Shirley turned to Clancy. "Can you let Red know where we are when he arrives?"

Clancy patted her arm. "The moment he gets here. Now, relax. I'll have somebody bring you something to write on and make sure you get situated." There was a rap at the door. Clancy yanked it open, startling a captain. "What is it?"

"Sorry to interrupt, Colonel, but General Goetsch wants to speak to you immediately."

Clancy cursed. "I had a feeling I'd be hearing from her. I just didn't think it'd be so soon."

The captain lowered his voice. "The shit's hitting the fan, sir. Our switchboard is lighting up. A lot of people want to talk to you. Apparently, there are at least seven dead at the hospital, and the locals want to know why a military unit went in and engaged the hostiles."

Clancy turned to Vanessa and Shirley. "If you'll excuse me, ladies, it looks like I have a lot of fires to put out."

Shirley nodded. "Of course, Colonel. And if you think us talking to anybody will help, just let us know."

"Thank you, ma'am." He bowed slightly then left the room, marching down the corridor, the captain on his heels. In retrospect, allowing the guys to take the Humvee was a mistake. It made it appear as if what they did was a military operation. Sending Dawson with Niner to the scene of his fiancée's kidnapping wouldn't be questioned by anyone, nor would Atlas accompanying Spock to the hospital. They had left in private vehicles, unarmed, though apparently Dawson had a weapon locked in his trunk.

Again, perfectly legal.

When Red had left with the others to help exfiltrate their people, they had their own private weapons, and only defensive gear from the armory. Again, something that wouldn't have been questioned if there hadn't been an engagement on the hospital grounds. Hindsight was always 20/20, and mistakes were often made in emergencies. If it had been a regular military op, they would address those mistakes during the debrief and post-op review, and lessons learned would be applied to future operations.

But this was different, and he would have a lot of explaining to do. Yet he had no regrets. His people weren't just the men and women under his command—it extended to their families, and both had been violated. And if he had it all to do again, he wouldn't hesitate. Now, he just needed to convince his superiors that he had made the right call.

He entered his outer office and pointed at the desk that Maggie normally sat at. "Get me the general," he ordered, and the captain sat behind the desk as Clancy entered his inner office, closing the door behind him. The intercom beeped.

"The general's on Line One, sir."

Clancy dropped into his chair and grabbed the receiver, pressing the flashing button, a verbal barrage greeting him the moment he was connected.

This might be a little tougher than I thought.

Kane/Lee Residence, Fairfax Towers

Falls Church, Virginia

CIA Operations Officer Dylan Kane rolled off the woman he loved, his chest heaving as he gasped for air. Lee Fang was always a bundle of energy in the sack, but today she had been particularly fierce. She draped herself over his chest, a leg straddling him, her own body covered in sweat.

"You let me know when you're ready for round two."

He chuckled, giving her a weak thumbs-up. "Roger Wilco. What the hell's gotten into you today?"

She propped her chin on his chest, staring into his eyes. "I missed you."

"I was only gone a week. I've been gone far longer than that before and you didn't nearly break me in half."

She shrugged. "Are you complaining?"

He grinned. "Hell no!"

She tapped his CIA-modified Tag Heuer watch. "Didn't you say you got a message?"

His eyes widened. "Oh shit, I forgot!" He pressed the buttons surrounding the crystal face in a coded sequence, and a message was projected indicating something had arrived through his private network from his former comrade-in-arms, Burt Dawson. Something must be wrong for him to be reaching out in this way. Dawson usually used official channels, so for him to make contact through the private network, it had to be something urgent.

And personal.

Fang picked up on his concern. "What is it?"

"It's from BD. I better reply."

Fang rolled off him and scurried up the bed, leaning against the headboard that had been rattling only moments before. "I have a feeling I'm not going to get my twelve rounds."

He swung his legs out of bed then twisted to give her a look. "Twelve?"

She flashed him a grin. "Don't worry, sweetheart, I was going to let you take breaks."

He rose. "Aren't you considerate." He looked about. "Where the hell are my pants?"

Fang giggled. "I don't think they made it past the front door."

Kane cursed and rushed out of the room for the front hall of their apartment, then sighed with relief that his pants had at least made it into the apartment, Fang attacking him the moment his key hit the lock. He reached down and grabbed the pants, then frowned as there was a tug on one of the legs.

Half of it was under the door.

He cursed and opened the door, pulling his pants inside. Someone gasped and he shot straight up, buck-naked, his cheeks burning at the elderly Mrs.

Jennings standing outside her door, her mouth agape, her eyes not staring at his face.

Or chest.

He quickly placed the pants in front of Dylan Jr. "Sorry, Mrs. Jennings. I…um…"

The old woman laughed, batting a hand at him. "I've seen worse, my dear."

He smiled weakly and stepped back into the apartment, closing the door, and he could have sworn he heard her say, "But never better." He headed back to the bedroom then sat, searching his pockets for his phone.

"Who were you talking to?"

"Mrs. Jennings. But I don't think she was really talking to me"

Fang's eyes narrowed. "Huh?"

He pointed at his kibbles and bits and Fang roared with laughter as he activated his secure messenger. He read the communique from Dawson and cursed.

"What is it?"

"Spock's wife Joanne has been murdered. BD's fiancée Maggie is missing, presumed kidnapped. He wants my help."

Fang rolled out of bed, heading to the closet. "Foreign or domestic?"

"Domestic." Kane fired back a message to Dawson.

Anything you need, I'm there.

Fang pulled out a go-bag and tossed it on the bed. "If it's domestic, can I come with?"

Fang was former Chinese Special Forces, living in exile in America. She was an elite soldier who was an asset on any mission, and he didn't hesitate. "Absolutely."

She squealed with glee and grabbed her own bag, tossing it beside his before heading to the shower. Kane sent a message to Chris Leroux, his best friend from high school, something that held true to this day.

I need you to pull as much information on this situation as possible.

He forwarded the message from Dawson and Leroux replied immediately.

I'm on it. Where are you?

In our apartment.

So are we.

We'll join you in 10 minutes.

Kane tossed the phone on the bed and joined Fang in the shower. Leroux was an Analyst Supervisor at the CIA and one of the best at his job. He and his team would pull any information there was to be known, and he'd have the answers shortly, his friend living in the same building as he now did. Fang stepped aside, freeing up the showerhead, and Kane turned his back to her as he soaped up, unwilling to risk arousal by her lithe body.

She smacked his ass before stepping out. "Hurry up."

A shiver rushed through him and he groaned. "Are you *trying* to delay us?"

She laughed. "You and your spanking."

He rinsed off then twisted the knob, the steaming hot water turning into icy needles, shocking any arousal out of him. He turned off the water and stepped out, grabbing a towel. "I told Chris we'd meet him at his apartment in ten. Let's find out what we're up against, then we'll reequip appropriately."

Fang was already in the bedroom. "Do you know if Sherrie's home?"

"His text said 'we' so I assume she is." He finished drying and joined Fang in the bedroom, finding a bra and panties already in place. Fang smiled at him. He could see the excitement in her eyes. She rarely got to see action due to her

66

status, and he was happy for her, though both of them would gladly have spent the weekend by themselves if it meant Maggie were safe and Joanne were still alive. He didn't know them well, but he had met them, being part of Bravo Team before his recruitment into the CIA. He knew Dawson and Spock well, and that was enough to mean he was dropping everything to help.

He stepped into a pair of underwear as Fang pulled a T-shirt over her head. "I hope Sherrie can help. It'd be fun to go on an op with her again."

Kane grunted, already working out what might have happened. Whatever was going on had to have occurred around Bragg. They weren't far from there, and if things got messy, they could get involved in the action, but he was well aware that wasn't what Dawson was looking for. He wanted intel, intel the CIA was best equipped to get. But there was a problem. They weren't supposed to operate domestically. He slipped his shirt on and buttoned it up then grabbed his phone, dialing the Chief, Leif Morrison. He was the National Clandestine Service Chief for the CIA and would be the one who would yay or nay the Agency's involvement.

And as the phone was answered at the other end, he was quite certain what the answer would be.

CIA Headquarters

Langley, Virginia

Leif Morrison sat at his desk, hunched over his keyboard, his back killing him. He closed his eyes and pulled off his glasses, tossing them on the desk before leaning back and stretching. He had to work on his posture, otherwise he would end up one of those old men with a pronounced hump that shuffled around his neighborhood. It was these damned computers. He was not a fan, though the technology allowed him to do incredible things.

He had started his career off as what the public would call a spy, but circumstances had pushed him toward administration, and now he was a director, formally the National Clandestine Service Chief. He loved his job, except for the paperwork and the constant reports coming in over his screen. In the past, it would be stacks of file folders. He'd grab one, lean back, and read it in comfort. But now it was all on the computer, which meant staring at a screen. And it was exhausting.

His phone beeped and he leaned forward, stabbing the intercom button. "Yes?"

"Dylan Kane for you, sir. Line One."

Morrison sighed, knowing full well what the call was about. He grabbed the receiver and hit Line One. "The answer is no."

Kane chuckled. "So, you're not going to refuse any request I make."

Morrison smiled slightly. Kane was arguably his best operative, but also one of his most unruly. He had to play this one carefully if he wanted to have any bit of control over what would happen over the coming hours and days. "Listen, Leroux already called me to get permission to use his team to look into what's going on in North Carolina."

"And you denied his request as well?"

"No, I did not deny him, however, I put limits. His team can provide background information on people identified by law enforcement, but they can't observe American citizens on American soil."

"So, basically what you're saying is they can run names and faces through a database, but those names and faces have to be provided to them?"

"Exactly."

Kane sighed. "Well, I guess it's better than nothing. Any chance you can spare Sonya Tong for a few days?"

This was where it got tricky. Morrison was aware Kane had set up his own off-the-books ops center somewhere in the region, but as long as he played ignorant, he had plausible deniability. "I'm pretty sure she has the weekend off, so I'm sure she's available for whatever social activity you have planned this weekend."

"Happy to hear it. And if you could keep Chris and Sherrie's schedule free for a few days, those social plans might just work out."

Morrison closed his eyes, tilting his head back as it slowly shook. "You kids have fun. Just try not to make the national news."

Kane laughed. "Who? Me?"

The call ended and Morrison hung up, wondering if he had done the right thing. If he was going by the book, he hadn't, but he had learned in this job the book was based on a world that wasn't real—it ignored the human element. A friend was dead, another was missing. There was no way he could stop his people from helping in any way they could. All he could do was limit the Agency's involvement while secretly cheering them on. The Russian mob was brutal, and a scourge the world over, but this time they had messed with the wrong people and were about to get far more than a bloody nose if he knew those now hellbent on revenge.

He groaned.

There's no way this isn't making the national news.

Leroux/White Residence, Fairfax Towers

Falls Church, Virginia

Kane knocked on the apartment door and it opened a moment later, a smiling Sherrie White greeting them then wagging the phone. "I just got a message that I'm out of rotation for three days. I assume I have you to thank for that?"

Kane shrugged as they stepped inside and joined their best friends in the living room. Leroux was attacking his laptop, his cellphone pressed to his ear, already doing what he was the best at—gathering information and interpreting the hidden meaning behind it. Kane dropped onto the couch and Fang sat beside him. Sherrie curled up on the love seat on the opposite side of the coffee table with Leroux. "So, what's the latest?"

Kane leaned forward. "I just got off the phone with the Chief. He basically said no CIA assets can be used to spy on American citizens on American soil."

Sherrie shrugged. "Well, we kind of expected that, didn't we?"

"Absolutely. But if we're going to find Maggie, we're going to need some sort of surveillance capability. We need access to traffic cameras, CCTV cameras from businesses in the area. Everything."

Leroux ended his call. "We need to open your facility."

Kane agreed. "That's exactly what I was thinking. The Chief already confirmed Sonya's not working until Monday."

Leroux tapped his phone. "I was just on with her. She's up for anything."

"Excellent, but we need more."

"I was thinking of bringing Tommy Granger back in. He's proved reliable and trustworthy."

"Make it happen. I want to be in Fayetteville in the next couple of hours. Can you get the ops center up and running by then?"

"I can be there. Sonya probably can as well. I'll contact Tommy right away and see if he can join us. I assume it's fully supplied?"

"Always."

"Then yes, we'll be set up before you arrive and hopefully have something for you. Are we passing any information on to law enforcement?"

Kane shook his head. "No. I don't want them getting wind that someone's working the case besides them. They might figure out who and get us shut down. I want to make this as easy on the Chief as possible. As far as he's concerned, we're all getting together to socialize."

Sherrie eyed him. "And he bought that?"

"He implied it, I ran with it. He just needs an alibi. Let's get the ops center set up. You start pulling as much footage as you can of the crime scene. See if you can trace where they might have taken Maggie. Sherrie, if you're up for it, we could use your skills on the ground."

Sherrie grinned. "I thought you'd never ask." She paused and glanced at her boyfriend. "Do you think there's any need for security at the ops center?"

Kane shook his head, answering for Leroux. "There shouldn't be. No one knows where it is besides us. If one of us is compromised, then we'll reevaluate that decision."

Sherrie smacked her hands together. "Then let's just make sure none of us is compromised." She leaned back. "So, we're going after the Russian mob?"

"Yes, and your ability to speak Russian could prove useful." Kane rose. "Let's meet out front in five minutes." He pointed at Leroux. "No hanky-panky, we're on a schedule."

Leroux flushed.

Sherrie winked. "Can we make it ten minutes?"

Kane stabbed a finger at her. "Five minutes. No fooling around."

Sherrie pouted. "Then that goes for you two as well."

Kane grinned. "We already got that out of the way."

Fang gave a toothy smile and Sherrie folded her arms, her lips shoved out. "That hardly seems fair."

Kane shrugged. "Sometimes you have to plan ahead." He made for the door. "Five minutes out front," he called over his shoulder. "Or we leave without you."

The Unit

Fort Bragg, North Carolina

Dawson stood in the ops center at the Unit, the team of professionals doing their best to coordinate with the locals, but it was mostly status monitoring—they weren't authorized to hack cameras. They had to rely on the locals for that, and they required warrants.

It was as frustrating as hell.

His phone vibrated with a message and he brought up Kane's secure app.

ETA two hours. Bringing a couple of friends. Should have full OTB-OC up and running before we arrive.

Dawson smiled. The CIA couldn't get involved. This was domestic. But Kane had his own facility, something his friend had set up just in case the system failed or it turned against him. It likely meant Leroux and others like him would be manning it, and that meant Maggie now stood a fighting chance—the pace things were moving at here, relying on the local authorities to save her, appeared certain to condemn her to death.

The door opened and Clancy entered. "Shut it down, people."

74

Dawson bristled but said nothing as the room turned toward their commanding officer, puzzled expressions on many of the faces.

"Sir?" asked the coordinator.

"General Goetsch has ordered us to leave this to the locals and not have any further involvement, so I want everybody to stand down from anything to do with tonight's incidents and return your full attention to ongoing operations."

"Understood, sir," replied the coordinator who turned to her people. "You heard the colonel. Shut everything down related to tonight's incidents."

Everyone returned their attention to their terminals as Clancy joined Dawson at the back of the room. "I'm sorry, son, but the general was pissed."

"Understood, sir. We weren't getting much done here anyway."

Clancy lowered his voice. "I assume you've made alternate arrangements?" He held up a hand. "Wait, don't tell me. I've taken your team out of the rotation for seven days. I recommend you all take some time to yourselves."

"Thank you, sir."

Clancy leaned in closer, lowering his voice further. "And Sergeant Major?"

"Yes, sir?"

"Whatever you're planning on doing, keep your faces off the evening news, otherwise, I won't be able to protect you."

"Understood, sir."

Clancy left the room and Dawson remained for a moment as various feeds went dark and his mind planned for what was to come. Kane would be here soon with help, and his skills could prove invaluable—especially at not getting themselves up shit's creek with the law. And the intel that Leroux could gather for them would be key to delivering justice—justice the system would have no part in. While their primary goal was the safe recovery of Maggie, once accomplished, he wanted revenge.

Bravo Team was going to war with the Russian mob.

Lightman Residence

Fort Bragg, North Carolina

Dawson sat outside Spock's house, debating whether he should send the message he had carefully crafted on his phone, detailing the events of the evening. If they were going to take on the Russian mob, they needed money. Kane apparently had a significant amount stashed away that he had accumulated over the years through gambling, the man an expert at reading people, always able to tell when they were bluffing. How substantial that fortune was, he had no idea, and he couldn't rely on it. But they were going up against the Russian mob, who certainly had access to substantial amounts.

He needed funding.

If this fight were to reach New York City, which he had no doubt it would due to how much time had passed, they would need plane tickets, vehicles, hotels, and possibly more. Not to mention illicit weapons.

He pressed *Send* and closed his eyes. He felt guilty for asking, but he had no choice. And as he sat waiting, watching the others arrive, he pictured Maggie and the last time they had been together. She had been excited about going out with her friends. He and the team had just returned from a mission, and because she worked for Clancy, he was the fortunate one of the team who got to see his better half before any of the rest. It was a brief stolen moment, but it was a good memory.

And if it were to be their last together, it was one he could live with.

He punched the dash and squeezed his eyes shut as his shoulders shook, the fear he had been holding back finally overwhelming him. His phone vibrated and he wiped his eyes dry then breathed a sigh of relief at the message he had just received from his friends, Archaeology Professors James Acton and Laura Palmer.

We are so sorry to hear about what happened. Our private jet network is at your disposal and $10 million has been placed in an emergency account. Details on how to access both will be sent through Dylan's messenger. If you want more, don't hesitate to ask. You're all family. Be safe and we love you all.

His app indicated a message had arrived. He opened it to find details on how to access his wealthy friends' lease-share network for private jets, and access the funds. He fired back a reply.

Details received. Thank you for your help. Will keep you posted.

They replied a moment later.

Good luck.

Dawson checked his eyes again then stepped out of the car. He headed into Spock's house, the humble military housing as packed as it had ever been, but emptier as well with Joanne's absence. They were all hurting, but they would soon have something to focus on, for now that he had secured funding and transportation, nothing was stopping the rampage about to begin.

Spock emerged from the hallway. "She's asleep." His mother eyed the team of Special Forces sitting in her son's living room, clearly displeased they hadn't left like the other guests. Spock picked up on it. "Thanks for helping out, Mom. I'll call you in the morning. The guys and I have something to discuss."

She frowned and turned to Dawson, wagging a finger at him. "Whatever you're planning, leave him out of it. He's got a daughter that needs him right now."

Dawson rose. "I can assure you, ma'am, your son will be remaining with his family."

Spock opened his mouth to protest but Atlas grabbed his wrist and squeezed, silencing him.

Mrs. Lightman eyed Dawson for a moment then frowned, taking a gentler tone. "I hope you find Maggie. She sounds like a sweet girl."

"She is, ma'am."

She hugged Spock then left, and the moment the door closed, Spock turned to Dawson. "You're not leaving me out of this."

Dawson held up a hand. "I meant what I said. Your place is here with your daughter, and your in-laws are arriving tomorrow. Your family needs you, and besides, right now the mission is to find Maggie and get her home safely. Once we've done that, we move on to phase two."

"Which is?"

"Retribution."

Spock sat on the arm of Atlas' chair. "There's no way you're keeping me out of that."

Dawson smiled. "I wouldn't dream of it. Now, here's the situation. Dylan will be here any minute with some help, and he's bringing an operations center of his own online. We should start to have good intel any minute now, and I've got even bigger news."

Spock leaned forward. "What's that?"

"The professors are funding us to the tune of ten million dollars, more if we need it, plus have given us access to their lease-share network."

Smiles broke out around the room, fist bumps and high-fives exchanged.

"There are no better people," rumbled Atlas, heads bobbing in agreement.

"I'm going to arrange a private jet at a nearby charter airport in case we have to leave the area."

"Do you think they've already left?" asked Niner.

Dawson nodded. "It's been hours, and if they know where we took Vanessa and Shirley, they know there's no way they're touching them. They're going to have to wait them out. The colonel said they can stay at the Unit for as long as they have to, but eventually they're going to have to leave. That's why I want to wrap this up as fast as we can. The colonel has given us a week, and all he's asked is that we stay off the news. That means we need to look civilian, but hide our identities, so here's what we're going to do. Everybody's going to go home, gather their personal gear, then we'll meet at my place. Dylan should be there by the time you get there. Spock, you stay here with your daughter. I need one volunteer to stay with them."

Sergeant Danny "Casey" Martin raised his hand. "It'd be my honor."

Spock shook his head. "No, you don't need to do that. I'll be fine."

"I know I don't need to, buddy, but I want to." Casey tapped his sidearm. "Besides, you need your sleep. You've got a big day tomorrow. I'll keep an eye on things."

Spock acquiesced. "Fine. And thank you."

Dawson rose. "Good. Everybody go home. Say your goodbyes, bring your gear, and every piece of weaponry you've got." He hesitated, holding out a hand, keeping everyone in their seats. He had to ask the question, though he was certain he already knew the answer. "We're about to get into some hairy shit, and I fully expect that by the time we're done, there's going to be a lot of dead Russians. Actions are about to be taken that some might claim are illegal rather than self-defense. We could get in shit. We could get completely hooped. Our careers could be over. If anyone wants to back out, no judgment here—just don't show up at my place, just stay home."

Niner opened his mouth to say something, but Dawson cut him off. "Nobody says anything. I don't want there to be any pressure. We're all going home, and if you're in, I'll see you at my place within the hour."

Everyone filed out in silence and Dawson gave Spock a thumping hug. "If you need anything, brother, you let me know."

Spock nodded and Casey patted him on the shoulder. "Don't worry, BD, he's in good hands. Now, you go find Maggie and stop worrying about us."

Dawson headed out the door and climbed into his Mustang, firing up the engine. This was a vigilante mission, and depending on how they played it, completely illegal. But if they were careful and only killed members of the Russian mob with minimal collateral damage, including no civilian injuries or deaths, and if they kept their identities reasonably hidden, no one would look too hard. But if things turned into a Charlie-Foxtrot, all their careers could be over, and they might spend the rest of their days in Leavenworth.

A price he was willing to pay as long as Maggie was safe when all was said and done.

Dawson/Harris Residence, Lake in the Pines Apartments

Fayetteville, North Carolina

Kane sat in Dawson's living room with Sherrie and Fang, half a dozen laptops spread out on the table, other tools of the trade laid out on the dining room table and kitchen counters. The doorbell rang and Kane rose, opening the door.

"I've got a delivery from Mr. Jones," said the man standing in the hall, wearing sunglasses and a ball cap pulled low.

"Bring it in here." Kane stepped aside, holding the door open. The man entered carrying two large duffel bags. He tossed them on the floor then stepped back into the hallway, grabbing two more, then another two.

"Everything I requested is there?"

"Yes, sir."

"Thank Mr. Jones for me."

"I will." The man walked down the hallway, passing Dawson as he came off the elevator.

Kane waved at his friend and smiled. "About time you got here."

Dawson returned a weak smile and stepped inside the apartment he and Maggie shared, and gave his friend a thumping hug. "Good to see you."

"How you holding up?" asked Kane as he stepped deeper into the apartment.

"As well as can be expected. Better now that you're here."

Sherrie and Fang rose and both gave Dawson hugs, expressing their condolences for the team's loss.

Dawson jerked a thumb at the six duffel bags. "What have we got here?"

"Everything a small army needs to take over an island nation."

Dawson smiled. "Perfect." He held out a hand toward the bags. "May I?"

"Of course."

Dawson grabbed the first one and unzipped it. He whistled. "MP5s."

"There are a couple of M4s in there as well, but I figured we'd be mostly close quarters. Flashbangs, grenades, explosives, surveillance equipment, drones. A little bit of everything, plus what we brought ourselves. If we need more, we can get it within an hour or two, wherever we happen to be."

Dawson chuckled. "For someone who's not supposed to be allowed to operate on American soil, you seem to be well connected in your homeland."

Kane shrugged as he sat on the couch, Sherrie and Fang sitting on either side. "You never know when your country is going to go mad and you may need to engage your own citizens to restore order. If that day ever comes, I want to know that I'm able to fight back." He regarded his friend. "How's Spock doing?"

Dawson took a seat across from him. "He seems to be holding things together, but I think that's just because he hasn't had a chance to be alone."

"Where is he now?"

"At home with his daughter. Casey's holding vigil."

"Good, he shouldn't be alone. What about the rest of the guys?"

"They should be here within the next half-hour. I've given them the option to bow out of what we're about to get into. Could be career-ending. Hell, it could be life-ending."

"If I'm going to go, I can't imagine a better way than trying to save one of our own."

"Amen," agreed Sherrie as Fang gave a firm nod.

"There's nothing more honorable than giving one's life for one's family," said Fang.

Dawson regarded them all for a moment then closed his eyes as he slumped forward in his chair. "You don't know how much it means to me that you're all here."

Kane ached for his friend. "You'd do the same for us." One of the laptops beeped and he reached forward, tapping on the screen. Leroux appeared and Kane smiled. "So, you're up and running?"

"Yeah, sorry for the delay. A logging truck jack-knifed, blocking the road here. It took a while for it to be cleared."

"Do you have a full complement?"

"Yes, Sonya and Tommy are here. All three of us will work for four hours, then we'll start alternating shifts just in case this is going to be a more extended op."

"Good thinking."

Sherrie leaned in and waved. "Hi, baby."

Leroux's cheeks flushed and he waved back. "Hi."

Kane bumped her out of frame with his shoulder. "Start pulling everything you can. You know what to do. Get back to us as soon you have something."

"Tommy and Sonya are already on it. Hopefully, we'll have something for you soon."

"Excellent. Good luck." Kane reached forward and ended the connection as someone knocked at the door. Dawson opened it, out of sight of the living room, and Kane smiled at Niner's voice, then Atlas', then more of the team he used to serve with. Within minutes, nine members of Bravo Team had joined them, every single one volunteering their careers, their futures, their lives, to help save a member of the family.

And it was moments like these when Kane missed the camaraderie of the Unit, and regretted his decision to go solo with the CIA.

Off-the-books Operations Center

Outside Bethesda, Maryland

Leroux took a seat at the bank of workstations lining one side of the heavily customized shipping container that was just part of Kane's secret setup. He had worked out of here several times before, including with Tong and Tommy Granger, a friend of the professors, someone who was an expert at computers and communications, and also, most importantly, trustworthy.

Though he still had to wear a hood on the way here.

"Status report."

Tong, normally his second-in-command at Langley when running an ops center, played her traditional role. "Everything is fired up and confirmed working. I also confirmed that our water, waste, refrigeration, and backup systems are functioning. We're good to go."

Leroux turned to Tommy who added his own update. "Confirmed. Everything is good. I've already entered the search parameters as you spec'd on the drive here. The unsecured camera database is starting to bring up hits of cameras that would have an angle on the target area. I'm going to start pulling archival footage. Hopefully, I'll have something for you in a few minutes."

"Excellent. Let me know the moment you have something. I need to get a target for the guys."

"You got it." Tommy went to work but multi-tasked. "Just what's the goal here?"

"To recover Maggie Harris."

"But aren't the police doing that?"

"I'm sure they are, but they're not as good as you, are they?"

"Hell no!"

"Exactly. And if that girlfriend of yours was kidnapped by the Russian mob, who would you want rescuing her? Local police or Delta?"

Tommy's fingers paused for a moment over the keyboard. "Delta, I suppose, but is that even legal?"

Tong chuckled. "Why do you think we're in here and not Langley?"

Tommy grunted, his fingers resuming their work. "Yeah, I guess I didn't think of that. Are we going to get in trouble for this?"

"Not unless you tell someone you were involved," said Leroux.

"Huh, I guess I shouldn't have made that posting on Facebook."

Tong and Leroux both turned in their chairs, staring at him.

Tommy continued to type. "You two are so easy." He paused. "Got something."

"Show me."

Tommy redirected the video to a larger display on the opposite wall. Leroux and Tong turned to watch a man straddling Maggie, a gun pointed at her head. He reached down and grabbed her by the shirt, dragging her to her feet. The man and his partner then led her into an alleyway where they lost sight of them, the camera angle from across the street only covering the entrance.

"Good, at least we know she was alive and that Vanessa was mistaken in thinking she had seen her getting shot. See if you can get another angle on the other end of that alleyway. I'm guessing they've got a vehicle nearby. If we can get a plate, we can trace it."

"Already on it."

Leroux sent a secure message to Kane.

MH confirmed alive, last seen entering alleyway with two hostiles.

"Now, let's just hope they kept her alive," he muttered.

Dawson/Harris Residence, Lake in the Pines Apartments
Fayetteville, North Carolina

Fist bumps and hugs were exchanged around the room as Kane shared the news that Maggie had left the scene alive. It confirmed the crime scene evidence, though contradicted what Vanessa thought she had seen—a muzzle flash. It meant the theory they were operating under, that Maggie was being held for intel purposes, was likely accurate. Dawson surveyed the room. Everyone to a man was here. Exactly as he had expected. They were a family, and family looked out for each other.

He raised a hand, bringing the celebration to a halt. "Let's start inventorying everything. I want to be ready to go the moment we have a location." He turned to Red. "I'll leave that in your hands."

"Yes, Sergeant Major." Red smacked his hands together. "You heard the sergeant major. Let's see what goodies we have."

Everyone went to work as Dawson sat across from Kane, Sherrie, and Fang. He leaned forward, staring at the carpet, taking a moment to absorb the news that Maggie hadn't been shot at the scene. She could still be dead, but there was now a chance she was alive, and with Leroux's team on the case, he was confident she would be found shortly.

Kane spoke into a headset as he worked several laptops, his words background noise. Dawson had to separate himself from the emotions that threatened to overwhelm him. He had to compartmentalize his fears and treat this like any other mission. Maggie wasn't his fiancée. She was his target that needed rescuing, like hundreds before.

Yet knowing what had to be done and actually doing it were two different things. He had never been so close to anyone before, and the thoughts of what could be happening to her consumed him. The Russian mob were brutal. They had no morals whatsoever. They wouldn't hesitate to beat her, to torture her, to rape her. He might rescue her tonight, but who he rescued might well be a completely different person.

He closed his eyes and sighed.

Sherrie leaned forward. "Are you okay?"

"Yeah." It was a lie, but he had to put on a brave face. He had to be strong. He had to be in control. This was his team, but if he couldn't maintain control, the responsible thing would be to hand everything over to Red. Yet Red had been through a lot as well. Shirley was all right, but traumatized, and the right place for him would be at her side. The same was true for Atlas. He should be with Vanessa. And the entire team was grieving for Joanne and Spock's family.

But they had a mission. There would be time to grieve later. Right now, minutes counted.

Kane raised a hand. "Quiet." The entire room stopped and Dawson leaned back, regarding his old friend. Kane tapped a key, putting the audio on speaker. "Repeat what you just said."

Leroux's voice replied. "We tracked the SUV back to a motel, just on the outskirts. Everyone, including Maggie, went inside."

"How long ago?"

"About fifteen minutes after the initial incident."

"Are they still there?"

"We don't know. We're having trouble accessing the feed, but they were there for at least forty-five minutes after their arrival. We backtracked the video and confirmed that the four hostiles you took out at the hospital came from that motel. That seems to be their base of operations."

Kane gave a thumbs-up to the room. "Okay, keep trying to access that footage. We need to know if they're still there, and if not, where they went."

"We're on it."

Dawson rose as the call ended. "Send the address to my phone. I want you three to stay here and coordinate things. It's been too long, so my guess is they won't be there, but we might get some clues as to where they went if they can't access the footage." He could tell Sherrie and Fang were disappointed to not get in on the action, but that wasn't his concern. It didn't faze Kane.

"No problem, BD. Good luck. I arranged a couple of SUVs. They're parked out front. Better you arrive in those than a bunch of Mustangs and Barracudas and whatnot." Kane tossed him two sets of keys.

Dawson caught the keys. "Good thinking." He tossed one set to Red. "Are we ready?"

"Yes, Sergeant Major. We're just waiting on you."

Body armor was tossed to Dawson and he geared up as everyone filed out of the apartment, Dawson bringing up the rear, his heart racing at what they might find. Would it be an empty motel room, or would they find Maggie's body, the Russians having cut their losses? A lump formed in his throat as he closed the door then headed for the stairwell, burying his fears and prepping for the mission.

And the horrifying possibilities it held.

Off-the-books Operations Center

Outside Bethesda, Maryland

Tommy cursed as he slammed a fist on the console. "I think I figured out what the hell is going on."

Leroux and Tong turned toward him. "What?" asked Leroux.

"Well, I just pulled the footage for the last few days, and every night at nine PM, the camera turns off. Nothing is recorded until six AM the next day."

Leroux's eyes narrowed. "What? Why would they do that? You would think at a motel, the most active time for problems would be at night."

Tong grunted. "Maybe that's exactly why they do turn it off. This is a no-tell motel. The customers probably wouldn't be very happy if they knew they were on camera."

"So, we've got a crooked night shift manager who's probably taking a payoff to turn off the cameras at night so that somebody can do business without being caught on tape, which means we're not going to get anything."

Tommy shook his head. "No, there's nothing to get."

"Okay, forget the motel cameras then. Find something else that has a shot of that parking lot. An ATM, CCTV, whatever. See if we can get a shot of them leaving or if they're still there. I want to be able to give them something before they get there."

"I'm on it."

Leroux turned to Tong. "How far a drive is it from Fayetteville to New York City?"

Tong tapped at her computer. "About eight to nine hours."

Leroux chewed his cheek for a moment. "If I'm Russian mob, and I find out a guy I've been looking for is in Fayetteville, I don't drive nine hours. I fly."

Tong agreed. "And I don't fly commercial because I'm coming heavily armed."

"Exactly. Run a check on charter flights from New York City to the Fayetteville area. Let's see if we can find anything unusual. And look for returning flights that either already left this evening or are about to leave. I have a feeling after losing five of their guys today, they're heading home to lick their wounds."

"You got it."

A pounding noise had all three of them freezing.

"What the hell was that?" asked Tommy, fear on his face.

Leroux rose and cocked an ear as the pounding noise resumed after a brief pause.

"Is that somebody at the door?" asked Tong.

Leroux snapped his fingers three times, pointing at the displays. "Bring up the door cam." Tong punched a button on her terminal and a camera showing the disguised entrance to their mini complex appeared, the greenish hues of the night vision camera revealing two men, one of them pounding on the door, the other standing watch.

"Is that a shotgun?" asked Tong.

Leroux's heart raced. It was. "Give me audio."

Tong flipped a switch.

"—know you're in there! Let us in and no one gets hurt!"

The pounding resumed.

"Who the hell are they?" asked Tommy. "How do they know we're here?"

Leroux shook his head. "Someone must have seen us come in."

"What do we do?" asked Tong.

Leroux pursed his lips as he thought. "Well, there's no way they're getting in here with a shotgun, but they could bring us unwanted attention." He repositioned his headset and contacted Kane.

"Hey, buddy, what's up?"

"We've got a problem."

En Route to Sleep Tite Motel

Fayetteville, North Carolina

Dawson had let Niner drive his team to the motel while Red and his took the other SUV. During the drive, Kane had sent him satellite footage of the motel showing what room Maggie had been brought into. It was a shithole, exactly the sort of place he would expect a hit team to temporarily set up in. It was a place where everybody minded their own business, and even if somebody saw something, they would never report it because they were probably doing something wrong themselves and wouldn't want the police showing up.

Unfortunately, the motel room that Maggie had been brought into by the two hostiles was small, with only one entry point. It was an unavoidable chokepoint, and they were going in blind. They had no idea if anyone was still in there since Kane's people hadn't found another camera angle showing the parking lot. They at least had a picture of the SUV the hostiles had arrived in. If it was no longer there, then they were likely about to hit an empty room. But there were no guarantees. Two hostiles had entered, but there was no way to know if there were any others still there, or how many might have left. They had to go in assuming they could come under fire the moment they breached the door.

And that the first shot wouldn't be at them, but at Maggie.

There was no room for error.

Red's voice came in over the comms. "Zero-One, Zero-Two. No sign of the subject SUV."

Dawson wasn't sure how he felt about that. It meant one of three things. Maggie was dead in the motel room, she had been taken somewhere else, or someone else had taken the vehicle. This new piece of intel was useless. "Copy that."

Niner pointed ahead. "There it is."

"Zero-Two, Zero-One. We're about to arrive. Have your team cover the rear."

"Roger that."

Niner shut off the lights and pulled into the parking lot, putting them directly in front of the room exactly as planned. All four doors opened at once, the team piling out. Atlas rushed ahead and swung the battering ram, the door tossed aside as he stepped out of the way. Dawson and Niner advanced, Glocks aimed forward. The bedside lamps were turned on, but as Dawson broke right, it was evident no one was here. Atlas and Mickey surged forward, clearing the bathroom and the closet, everyone shouting, "Clear!"

Dawson activated his comms. "Zero-Two, Zero-One. The room is secured and empty, over."

"Copy that."

"Zero-Two, I want your team to stand down and head to rendezvous point Alpha."

"Roger that."

Dawson observed as his men searched the room, every detail planned on the way here. Red's team was already leaving the area now that they weren't needed. The last thing they wanted was somebody reporting heavily-armed men running around a shady motel.

"I've got something." Atlas held up a trash bin. "Russian cigarettes and a matchbook for a bar in New York City. Diggler's. Looks like some sort of strip joint."

"Bring them with us."

Niner turned to Dawson. "I've got something here." His voice was subdued.

"What is it?"

Niner pointed at a chair sitting in a corner. Dawson walked over, his stomach turning at the sight of blood on the floor and on the walls. It appeared someone had been placed in the chair then beaten.

And that someone had to be Maggie.

Atlas placed a massive hand on his back. "Even if it was her, there's hardly any blood here. That means they didn't kill her. She left here alive."

Dawson drew a deep breath, nodding. Atlas was right. She had been beaten by her captors, probably to get her to reveal the identities of the other women that were with her. This was actually good news. It extended the timeline in which she was alive. But it also enraged him.

Whoever was responsible had to die.

Gruesomely.

Off-the-books Operations Center

Outside Bethesda, Maryland

Leroux put a comforting hand on Tommy's shoulder, though he could use some comforting himself. The pounding outside continued, sometimes the butt of the shotgun used in place of the fist. "Just focus on your work." He pointed to the noise-canceling headphones Tommy always brought with him. "Put those on. You need to find out where they took Maggie."

Tommy nodded then reached out with two trembling hands. He fit the headphones in place then took a long drag on his insulated cup's straw. The young man went back to work and Leroux turned in his chair to face Tong.

"Bring up the other external cameras. I want to know where these guys came from. We've never had a problem here before, and this is a private lot."

Tong brought up half a dozen angles, splitting them on the large screen on the opposite wall.

"Run them back to when we arrived here."

All six cameras began reversing, their time codes counting down.

"Wait a minute. Bring up camera five."

Camera 5 quickly filled the screen and Leroux pointed to the top left corner. "Is that what I think it is?"

Tong isolated the area and it zoomed in to fill the screen, the software enhancing the image. "If you mean does it look like a beat-up Winnebago that belongs in Clark Griswold's driveway, then yeah."

Leroux cursed. "What the hell is that doing here?" It was tucked between two containers, only the front of it visible because of the camera angle. Unless someone went up and down the lot, they would never spot it.

"Squatters?" suggested Tong.

"Could be. Certainly trespassers. The question is, are they here for the night, or have they been here long-term?"

"It doesn't matter. They're here now, and they're a problem."

Leroux sighed. "They're only a problem if they get inside, and there's no way that's happening. The skin of the containers has been reinforced. They'd need a rocket launcher to make a dent in it."

The hard pounding of the shotgun butt startled them both as it now came from overhead. Leroux snapped his fingers. "Roof cam, now!"

Tong flipped a switch and they got a low-angle view of the roof as the trespasser with the shotgun, now overhead, hammered away at one of the exhaust ports to their HVAC system.

Leroux frowned. "Okay, *now* we have a problem."

Tong's eyes drifted to one of the lockers on the far wall containing a host of weaponry. "Do you know how to shoot a gun?"

Leroux shrugged. "Basic CIA training like you had, plus Sherrie's been teaching me. But I'm not about to go and shoot two guys who are probably just drunk."

"What if they get in here?"

"Well, that's a different story. Then it's self-defense."

Tommy tore his headphones off and turned in his chair. He opened his mouth when more pounding from overhead had the blood draining from his face. "What the hell was that?"

"One of them's on the roof," explained Tong.

He noticed the image on the screen and gasped. "We have to do something. If he starts messing with things up there, we could lose communications or power. Any number of things."

"There's not much we can do," said Leroux. "We'll cross that bridge when we come to it." He focused on the job at hand. "Did you find something?"

Tommy continued to stare at the image as the pounding echoed overhead.

"Tommy, focus!"

Tommy's stare jerked back to Leroux. "Yeah, right." He shook his head and turned back to his terminal. "I found the SUV on a camera heading north. It left about fifteen minutes after the team was hit at the hospital."

Tong glanced at Leroux. "They must have missed a check-in."

Leroux agreed. "Can you see where they're heading?"

Tommy tapped a map on the screen. "I'm still tracing them, but there's an airport in that direction."

Tong spun in her chair, resuming the work interrupted by their uninvited guests. "What's the name of the airport?"

"Fayetteville Regional."

She brought it up. "I've got a flight that left for New York City an hour ago from there."

"And when did it arrive?"

"This afternoon."

"Who chartered it?"

"That's going to take some time, but I think it's safe to say someone with Russian mob connections."

"See if you can get us some footage of that," Leroux said to Tommy.

"On it."

Tommy gave one last glance at the roof then put his headphones back in place, attacking his keyboard as Tong continued to work. A huge bang, unlike anything they had heard yet, rang out overhead and Leroux spun in his chair to see their intruder reloading his shotgun. Tommy had sensed the shot and paused momentarily, peering around before resuming his work.

Leroux rose and placed a hand on Tong's shoulder. "Just keep working. He's not getting in here with a shotgun. The more ammo he wastes, the better."

She nodded, but he could feel her entire body shaking. They were analysts. They weren't supposed to be under fire. They were supposed to be working in the safety of Langley, where the only way they would ever be under fire was if something went horribly wrong with their country.

Another gunshot and Leroux headed for the cabinets, opening them all, revealing an array of handguns, submachine guns, and assault rifles. He pulled two Glocks and six mags. He loaded them both, then placed one at his workstation and one beside Tong, along with the spare magazines. She paused what she was doing, staring at the weapon for a moment, then resumed her work as Leroux jacked back into his console and contacted Kane to give him an update on the situation. The two idiots outside had to be stopped before they damaged something that affected their op.

And simply going outside and killing them wasn't an option.

Unfortunately.

Fayetteville Regional Airport

Fayetteville, North Carolina

Dawson sat in the SUV, staring through his binoculars, surveying the small airport the charter they believed carrying Maggie and her hostage-takers had departed from. It, coincidentally, was the airport where the charter for the professor's private jet was supposed to be waiting for them, but it had already departed on a priority mission. He punched the dash as he lowered the binoculars, his frustration mounting.

Niner turned toward him from the driver's seat. "You have to look at this from the positive side."

Dawson eyed him. "Oh?"

"If they intended to kill her any time soon, they wouldn't have taken her on the plane."

Dawson frowned. Niner was right, but it didn't mean she was safe. They already had evidence she had been beaten badly enough for blood to be drawn and for information to have been given up. They could be doing unspeakable things to her worse than death, and the thought filled his mouth with bile.

His phone rang and he checked the display. He didn't recognize the number. He swiped his thumb, taking the call. "Hello?"

"This is Detective Samuel. I assume I'm speaking to Sergeant Major Dawson?"

"Yes, Detective," he said, silencing the others.

"I'm at the Sleep Tite Motel. Ever heard of it?"

Dawson trod the line between the truth and a lie. "Should I have?"

"Well, we traced a vehicle that was used to take your fiancée from the crime scene to this motel, and imagine my surprise when I get here and find the door broken open, the room searched, and guests telling me that a bunch of men dressed as if they were auditioning for a James Bond movie hit the place not fifteen minutes ago."

Dawson said nothing. He was just thankful they had vacated the area as quickly as they had.

"Where are you now, Sergeant Major?"

"I'm with members of my unit, mourning our loss."

"You wouldn't happen to be out chasing the Russian mob, would you?"

Dawson ignored the question. "Have you made any progress in finding my fiancée?"

"As I said, we traced a vehicle to this motel, but it's no longer here. We'll continue to trace it. We will find your fiancée, but we need you to stand down and stop interfering."

"Understood, Detective." Dawson ended the call. "They just got to the motel. Witnesses saw us and he's not happy. He wants us to stand down."

Niner shook his head in disbelief. "He wants us to stand down, yet he just got to the motel?"

Dawson stared at the airport ahead. "They're only fifteen minutes behind us, so we're not doing that much better."

"Yeah, but they don't know about the airport or the flight, now do they?"

Dawson punched the dash again. "Of all the nights, why the hell did two drunks have to interfere?"

"What do we do now?"

Dawson tossed his phone on the dash. "We wait for our plane to get back"

Niner eyed him. "Couldn't we just ask for another one?"

Dawson twisted in his seat. "What do you mean?"

Niner shrugged. "It's a lease-share *network*. She has a portion of a fleet. Can't we just ask for another plane?"

Dawson cursed. "I never thought of that." He grabbed his phone and made the call.

En route to the off-the-books Operations Center

Outside Bethesda, Maryland

Sherrie downshifted as they reached a sharp bend in the road. She killed their speed then accelerated out of the turn as Fang expertly guided a drone along their path, about half a mile ahead, watching for any obstacles including police. She didn't expect any speed traps, not at this time of night, not in this area—it was too sparsely populated—but a random officer on patrol could cause problems.

Their plane had just landed, Kane having dispatched them the moment he heard of the two drunks attempting to gain access to his ops center. It had been over an hour since her boyfriend's call, and the last check-in indicated things had escalated.

She redialed Leroux's number.

"Hello?"

"Status?"

"I was just about to call you. The guy on the roof is still trying to shoot off one of the ventilation covers, but the other guy is more of a concern now. He returned to his RV and just came back with what looks like cutting equipment. He's got some sort of blowtorch."

Sherrie cursed and pressed the accelerator a little harder. This no longer sounded like drunks, but it also didn't sound like something planned. She took another sharp S curve as her CIA-trained mind struggled to figure out just what was going on. "Is he showing any signs of progress?"

"Hard to tell. The torch is so bright when it's active that the night vision is knocked out. It looks like he's trying to cut out the keypad and access the wires inside, I guess."

"He'd still have to know what to do even if he got to that point," said Fang.

"Tommy agrees with you," replied Leroux. "But he also says that sheer dumb luck could have them opening the door."

"Are you armed?" asked Sherrie.

"Sonya and I have Glocks at our stations. Tommy's not trained."

"Good. Here's what you do. Just like in your training, remember that there's no safety switch on the Glock, so don't waste any time looking for one. It's built into the trigger. If he comes in, just aim at center mass. That means aim at his chest and you keep firing until he stops moving. Don't try to hit him in the arm or the leg to just wound him, don't try to go for the fancy head shot. Police training. Aim center mass, keep shooting until the target stops moving. That means they're no longer a threat."

There was a pause before Leroux replied. "Let's hope it doesn't come to that. How far out are you?"

Sherrie glanced at the navigation system. "Ten minutes."

Leroux cursed. "He's got the panel off."

"His friend's climbing down from the roof," came Tong's voice in the background.

"Can you block that door with anything?" asked Fang.

"I'll take a look and see. Let's just hope that blind, dumb luck is on our side tonight and not theirs. Just get here as fast as you can."

Sherrie glanced at the dash. "Nine minutes. Just remember what I said. Stay calm, center mass, keep shooting until the target stops."

"But there are two targets."

"Don't worry about that. The guy with the gun is going to go in first, and he's the biggest threat. Just immediately open fire. Don't hesitate, just keep shooting, and when he's down, his friend is going to either run away or have already run away. These don't sound like professionals. They're not there to get you. They've just stumbled upon something and they want what's inside, not who's inside."

"Okay, I'm going to let you go now. I'll keep you posted on what's happening."

"Copy that," said Sherrie, and the call went dead. "How am I looking ahead?"

"Still clear," replied Fang as she controlled the drone.

"What's the range on that thing?"

Fang shrugged. "It's satellite, so if the battery lasts long enough, Beijing?"

Sherrie chuckled. "I've got an idea."

En Route to New York

"I don't think she even shed a tear," boomed Atlas from the rear of the Gulfstream V the team was now on. "Vanessa's one tough woman." The pride in the man's voice was obvious. Gone was the concern from earlier.

"She is one tough cookie," agreed Niner. "Tougher than her boyfriend."

Atlas eyed him. "What the hell are you talking about?"

"Are you forgetting that I was there the first time you were shot? You cried like a baby."

"I did no such thing."

"Sure you did. You had tears running down your face. I don't blame you. If I got shot in the ass like you did, I might shed a tear as well. But hey, I'm not the tough guy you are."

Atlas stabbed a meaty finger at the diminutive Niner. "Hey, shedding tears because of intense pain is completely different than being a blubbering idiot."

"Are you implying something?"

Red switched seats to be closer. "Wait a minute. When Spock dropped that fifty cal on your foot last year, you were hopping all over the place, grabbing your foot, and tears were rolling down your cheeks."

Niner fired him a look. "Those were tears of disappointment, not pain."

Red's eyes narrowed. "Disappointment?"

"Yeah, we were about to leave on a mission. I got scrubbed."

Atlas shrugged. "Well, your foot did balloon to the size of a volleyball."

Jagger chuckled. "I forgot about Wilson. That puppy was nasty looking."

Niner agreed. "That hurt worse than getting shot. I wish Spock was here, I'd punch him again."

Jagger frowned. "Poor bastard would probably appreciate the distraction."

Niner sighed. "Hopefully we get Maggie back tonight, then kill every last one of the bastards involved. Knowing they're dead will hopefully bring him some comfort."

"I just hope we get to Maggie in time," said Atlas, his deep voice carrying the length of the plane. The team fell silent out of respect for Dawson. "Sorry, BD."

Dawson flicked a wrist, dismissing the unnecessary apology, instead flagging the flight attendant. He had been on private jets before, but typically they were operated by the American military, so the sexy blonde in the short skirt offering a full open bar was not what he and his team were accustomed to. He had already given instructions that no alcohol was to be served, the men groaning and protesting, though only in jest.

This was a mission, and everyone had to be sharp.

She brought him an ice-cold bottle of water. "Can I get you anything else?"

He shook his head. "Just an exact ETA from the pilot."

She pointed at the display at the front. "It's been my experience that that's extremely accurate, but I'll confirm it with the pilot."

"Thank you."

When they arrived didn't really matter. The Russians were already on the ground. Kane sat across from him, reduced to one laptop as he dealt with the crisis at his ops center. Kane's team was still working the op as best they could, though he had no doubt they were distracted. Leroux and Tong might be CIA, but they weren't properly trained for these types of things, and Tommy was just a civilian. A kid.

Dawson closed his eyes. A kid. He wanted to have kids with Maggie. If something happened to her, if she were to die tonight, that dream was dead, along with her. The pain would be too great to ever let his heart expose itself again. Maggie was the last woman he was ever going to love. She was his last chance at a family, and if he lost her, all those plans were finished. He would honor her memory until the day he died, and it scared him that deep down, if things were to turn bad, and the worst were to happen and she were found dead, he wanted to die along with her, taking down as many of the enemy as he could.

Niner dropped in the seat beside him. "How are you doing?"

Dawson took a swig of his water, his Adam's apple bouncing as he kept drinking, delaying the need for a response. He finally stopped, putting the cap back on the bottle. "I'll be fine." He leaned forward and stared across at Kane. "Do we have a destination yet?"

Kane shook his head as the cabin settled down and gathered around them. "We've confirmed the plane landed at Teterboro Airport in Jersey. We're trying to get some footage to see what vehicle they got in. Tommy thinks he should have something in the next few minutes."

"Do we know who that plane belongs to yet?"

Kane held up his hand and tipped it from side to side. "Sort of. Sonya's tracked it back to a holding company. She's trying to determine the ownership. My guess is it'll be buried several layers deep. Hopefully, by the time we're on the ground, we'll have a name and a destination."

Atlas pointed at the clock counting down at the front of the cabin. "Are we landing at the same airport?"

Dawson shook his head. "No, the flight plan was already filed, and the pilot told me when we boarded that it couldn't be changed in mid-air on such a short flight. Besides, our rental vehicles are all waiting for us there. Any travel time will just allow us to properly plan an assault. If this is Russian mob, I fully expect them to be in some sort of well-defended compound."

Atlas held up his phone. "There are airports closer to the city. For them to land here makes me think we're going to some country estate and not a downtown apartment."

Red shook his head. "I wouldn't read too much into that. They could land and board a chopper that'll put them on the roof of a building downtown in twenty minutes."

Kane cursed. "I didn't think of that." He activated his comms, feeding Leroux this new theory, asking him to find out about any choppers that might have left the airport after the Russians had arrived.

Dawson pointed at the display. "We're going to be on the ground in fifteen minutes. Everybody use the bathroom. Do whatever you need to do. Make sure you're ready to hit the ground running. And don't forget your ball caps and keep your heads down. I promised the colonel we wouldn't make the news, but I didn't promise him what we're about to do wouldn't."

Off-the-books Operations Center

Outside Bethesda, Maryland

Leroux stood at the entrance to the control center, his Glock aimed down the corridor toward the door. His hand was shaking despite his left supporting his right. He wasn't cut out for this. It was one thing to know how to shoot a gun, it was another thing to know you're about to kill someone, someone who might be an asshole, who might be a drunk or a drug addict, but someone who was a human being, who on an ordinary day might be a perfectly good person. This wasn't the North Koreans or the Chinese attempting to break in. These weren't Muslim terrorists or even the Russian mob. But he had no choice. If the door was breached, they had to die. It was him and his people, or the two intruders.

He just prayed it didn't come to that.

The camera revealed that one of them was randomly touching wires together, as if hotwiring a car, and not sixty seconds ago, an alarm on their console had sounded, indicating the seal on the door had been momentarily disabled. And for that brief moment, until the man had moved on to another wire combination, all they had to do was push the door and it would have opened.

He had nearly soiled himself.

He glanced over at the others. Tong was shaking almost uncontrollably as she continued to work. Tommy had his noise-canceling headphones on and was tracing back various cameras, though his foot was tapping furiously, his nerves rattled as well.

Leroux stared at the door. He had managed to take a cot from the sleeping quarters and jam the metal frame between the fold in the metal door and the fold in the wall of the container. It might delay them for a few seconds or a few minutes. He had no idea how quickly the metal of the cot would give way, though even if it were only a few seconds, it would hopefully give him enough time to calm his nerves then take aim. It was critical he got the first shots off, but it was more critical that his aim was true.

He glanced back at the monitor, something catching his eye. The man with the shotgun was aiming at the sky. He fired a round and his partner, playing with the exposed locking mechanism, stopped what he was doing. Leroux adjusted his headset then dialed Sherrie.

"Hello, my love."

"Can I assume that we have you to thank for what's happening?"

"Well, it was my idea, but you'll have to thank Fang for the implementation."

"What's your ETA?"

"Four minutes."

"Son of a bitch!" cried Fang in the background.

"What happened?" asked Leroux. He stared at the screen to see the shotgun lowered, its handler leaving the frame then returning a moment later with the remnants of the drone. Leroux cursed.

"The guy's a better shot than he looks," said Sherrie. "Sit tight, we'll be there in three minutes. Hopefully, that bought us a little bit of time."

Leroux frowned. "Or it just made them more determined to get in here. I'm going to hang up. Make sure you call me first before you come through the door. I'm feeling a little trigger-happy right now."

Sherrie laughed. "Wouldn't that be ironic? After all the missions I've been on, I get taken out by my own boyfriend!"

Leroux smiled slightly. "Well, we can always hope my training has been woefully inadequate."

Both women roared with laughter. "See you soon, sweetie. Don't shoot anything with boobs."

The call ended and Leroux frowned as the pounding on the metal door resumed, the butt of the shotgun once again employed, the other man continuing his random efforts that had already worked once. And if they worked again, his partner's hammering on the door might just reveal that fact to them when it swung open from one of the blows.

He checked the clock on the wall, counting down the seconds in his head until the arrival of their saviors.

Please God, don't let anything slow them down.

En route to the off-the-books Operations Center

Outside Bethesda, Maryland

Fang braced against the dash as Sherrie hammered on the brakes then cranked the wheel, sending them into a controlled skid as they finally arrived at the secluded storage area containing Kane's off-the-books operations center. Fang released her death grip on the dash then rechecked her weapon as Sherrie guided them through the maze of containers and vehicles. She turned off the lights and slowed. Fang lowered her window and tilted her head outside. Someone was shouting, an angry man pounding something hard against metal, each blow punctuating his incoherent rants.

Sherrie brought them to a halt. "How do you want to play this?" she asked as they both stepped out of the car.

Fang shrugged as they made their approach. "If this were China, I'd simply shoot the two of them then call for a disposal crew."

Sherrie grunted. "Fortunately for them, this isn't China."

Fang sighed as she pressed against the back of one of the containers housing the operations center. "You Americans are too soft on crime."

"I think you'll find the country is rather divided on that." Sherrie waved at one of the hidden cameras, blowing a kiss to Leroux. "We only shoot if they shoot first."

"Yeah, well, they could get lucky with that first shot."

"True." Sherrie grinned. "But I bet you they wouldn't shoot a naked woman."

Fang's eyes shot wide. "Excuse me?"

"Take your clothes off. It'll distract them long enough for me to disarm the guy with the shotgun."

Fang pointed at Sherrie's ample bosom then at her own. "Molehills. Those mountains distract men more than these things."

Sherrie giggled. "Fine." She handed over her Glock and Taser then quickly stripped bare. She struck a pose for the camera and Fang could only imagine what Leroux was thinking. They split up, taking opposite sides of the container, the shouting and pounding growing louder as Fang approached the far end.

"Howdy, boys. Anyone looking for a good time?" said Sherrie from the opposite side of the container.

Fang shook her head though couldn't help but smile as she emerged to see the two men with their backs to her, staring slack-jawed at the stunning Sherrie. The shotgun was aimed at the ground, held by the man on her right. Fang squeezed the Taser's trigger, sending an excruciating amount of voltage into the man's back. He involuntarily squeezed the trigger of the shotgun, blasting a shell harmlessly into the ground. His partner yelped then spun around as Fang cleared her throat, aiming the Glock squarely at his chest. She tossed Sherrie a zip tie and the CIA operative bound the man's hands behind his back then patted him down. Finding nothing other than his wallet, she shoved him to his knees then patted down the still gurgling Taser victim, relieving him of his wallet, a handful of shotgun shells, and a switch blade. Fang handed over another zip tie and Sherrie put it to use then stood back, admiring their handiwork as Fang cleared the shotgun.

A voice came over a hidden speaker. "I think you can put your clothes on now." It was Leroux.

Sherrie grabbed the girls and did an alternating bounce for the benefit of the camera. "Are you sure?"

"You do realize there are others in here."

Sherrie batted a hand. "Nothing they haven't seen before."

Leroux's reply had them both in stitches. "I would hope they haven't seen *yours* before."

Sherrie flashed a wink at Fang. "I guess I'd have to know who's in there."

Leroux groaned then became serious. "What now?"

Sherrie stared at the two men. "Well, I'm going to get dressed, then we're going to pay a visit to their RV and have a little talk."

"Understood."

Sherrie disappeared as Fang stood watch, disappointed at how smoothly things had gone. She was hoping for some action, but unfortunately, the car ride here where she was merely a passenger was the most exciting part of this encounter. Firing a Taser was hardly exhilarating. Sherrie reappeared, returning the scene to a PG rating, and Fang handed back her Glock. Sherrie flicked it.

"Okay, boys, get up."

The two prisoners struggled to their feet, and Fang got her first good look at them. They were young.

"Now, why don't we check out that lovely RV of yours. I hear it's Christmas Vacation worthy."

They scowled but began their shuffle deeper into the storage yard. They walked between two rusted containers then turned left. Just ahead, Fang spotted the nose of a beat-up green and white Winnebago. Sherrie pressed the barrel of her gun against the tased man's testicles.

"Is there anyone else inside?"

He shook his head.

"If you're lying to me, you'll be singing soprano for the rest of your life."

His eyes narrowed. "I didn't know they sang on that show."

Sherrie rolled her eyes at Fang, though she was even more in the dark than their prisoner. Sherrie flicked her weapon again. "Both of you, face down on the ground." Muttered curses were the response as they awkwardly dropped to their knees, made difficult by their bound hands. She glanced at Fang. "You watch them. I'll clear the vehicle."

Sherrie advanced toward a rusted screen door midway down the RV. Fang repositioned to be halfway between the door and their prisoners. Sherrie pulled open the screen door, stepped aside, and listened. Fang did as well, her heart beating a little quicker, enjoying the touch of extra adrenaline surging through her veins. She wasn't concerned. The attempt to gain entry to the ops center had been going on for over an hour. If they had friends, the friends would have joined them by now.

Sherrie stepped forward, the pneumatic spring pressing the filthy screen against her back as she entered, her Glock in one hand, her flashlight in another, coupled together. She disappeared inside and Fang resisted the urge to hold her breath, instead controlling her breathing, and listening while keeping an eye on their prisoners.

"Well, forget Christmas Vacation, this is more Breaking Bad," came Sherrie's voice from inside.

Fang perked up. She loved Breaking Bad and had binge-watched it and Better Call Saul too many times to count. "You mean it's a meth lab?"

Sherrie appeared in the doorway. "Well, they're cooking something, and it ain't chili, but I'm not convinced they know what they're doing." She stepped down to the ground then walked over to the two prisoners. "So, let me guess, you two geniuses watched a little too much Netflix and decided you could do it too?"

The men said nothing, their faces still pressed into the ground.

"How long have you been here?"

Again, nothing.

Sherrie booted the shotgun-toter in the ribs and he groaned. "Answer me, or she starts cutting."

Fang drew her knife and flipped it in the air, catching it by the blade, then smiled. "I was hoping to get to use this tonight."

The man's eyes bulged. "Two days! We got here two days ago!"

Sherrie tossed the wallets to Fang then drew her weapon, aiming it at the men. "Why don't you tell me who we have here?"

Fang pulled the IDs. "We have Billy Donahue and Clay Fuller, both hailing from Bethesda. And look at this, both only twenty years old."

Sherrie tsked at them. "Not even old enough to drink, but old enough to cook meth. Your parents must be very proud. Now, let me tell you what's going to happen. The two of you are going to get in that piece of shit, you're going to drive out of here, and you're going to forget everything that happened tonight." She gestured at the IDs Fang was holding. "We're going to keep those. And the friends we work for are going to let you live as long as no one comes around here asking questions." She kneeled at the head of the tased man and lifted his chin with the barrel of her gun. "Have you watched Breaking Bad?"

"Y-yes."

"Then you'll understand this. She and I are the Salamanca twins. So, you know what that means?"

"You work for the cartel?"

"Exactly. Screw with us, and I guarantee you no one will ever remember your name. You got me?"

The man nodded, tears flowing.

She drew her knife and cut the zip ties off both of them then stepped back. "Now, get the hell out of here, and don't let me ever see your faces again." They scrambled to their feet and, moments later, the RV lurched out of the lot and onto the road. She turned to Fang. "Well, that was fun."

Fang shrugged. "I suppose. Definitely better than sitting on the couch, watching dramas about the decline of American society."

Sherrie holstered her weapon. "If you're looking to watch something, then I suggest The Sopranos and Christmas Vacation, if you haven't seen it yet."

Fang groaned. "Dylan's already made me watch that one every Christmas that we've known each other."

Sherrie stared at her. "And you don't love it?"

Fang shrugged. "I think you have to understand the cultural references to enjoy that movie."

Sherrie regarded her firmly. "I'm not sure we can be friends anymore."

Fang's eyes shot wide and her chest ached. "Why not?"

Sherrie shot forward and hugged her hard. "I'm so sorry, I was just joking!"

Fang hugged her back then gently pushed her away. Sherrie smiled, tears in her eyes.

"I'm sorry. Sometimes I forget you don't always get my sense of humor."

Fang relaxed, surprised at how much the misunderstanding had hurt, and it made her realize just how far she'd come. This was her home. These people were her friends and family, and she wasn't sure how she felt knowing her former home was a place she had put behind her.

Her chest ached for an entirely different reason.

Leroux opened the outer door and smiled at Sherrie and Fang as they stepped inside. Sherrie gave him a kiss that had him weak in the knees, the woman always insatiable after a mission. He broke the lip lock and took a step back. "Your mission might be over, but I'm still in the middle of mine, so don't start anything we can't finish."

Sherrie patted Little Chris, who had already shown interest. "Tell him that."

He grunted.

Fang shook her head. "You two are ridiculous."

Leroux gave her a look. "Don't blame this on me."

"Right, like you're innocent."

Leroux flushed then stepped outside, examining the damaged security panel. He shook his head, cursing. "Dylan is going to have to bring someone in to fix this. Thank God there's a manual override on the inside, otherwise we could be stuck in here." He closed the door and the three of them entered the small operations center. Tommy continued to work furiously, his noise-canceling headphones still in place, while Tong turned to greet their guests.

"So, what was it?" she asked, the relief in her voice obvious.

Fang batted a hand. "Just a couple of meth heads. Their Winnebago was a lab."

"Are they going to be a problem?"

Sherrie shook her head. "I don't think so, but this location has been compromised. Dylan might want to relocate after this op."

Leroux dropped into his chair and muttered a curse. "He's not going to be happy about that."

Sherrie looked around. "How much do you think it would cost to move something like this?"

Leroux shrugged. "The units are pretty much self-contained and are designed to be moved. It's finding a new secure location that you can trust where questions won't be asked, and arranging all the hookups. That's the problem." He sighed. "Well, not *my* problem."

Sherrie checked her watch. "Where are the boys?"

Leroux jerked a thumb toward the large screen behind the two women. "They've just landed in New York City."

"Do we have a destination for them?"

Leroux tapped Tommy on the shoulder. Startled, he ripped the headphones off. "Okay, we need to figure out something other than physically touching me, otherwise Mai's going to need to bring me more underwear."

Leroux eyed him. "And just what would you suggest? Flick the lights?"

"Or you could just not wear the headphones," smirked Tong.

Tommy cocked an eyebrow then flinched again when he finally noticed Sherrie and Fang standing behind him. "When did you get here?"

"We're not here. Weren't you told?" replied Sherrie, straight-faced.

"Huh?"

"You're too easy, sweetie," laughed Sherrie as she tousled his hair. "We just came in a minute ago."

"Oh…oh! What happened to those two guys?"

"Fang tased one of them, I threatened to shoot his balls off, and then after putting the fear of God into both of them, they left."

Tommy pulled at the collar of his Atari t-shirt. "Will they be coming back?"

"They shouldn't be."

"Shouldn't?" Leroux bit his lip as he thought for a moment. "I know the plan was for you to fly back to New York, but maybe that's not the best idea."

Sherrie regarded him. "You want us to stay here?"

"I don't know if it's necessary for both of you to stay, but at least one."

Fang raised a finger. "I'll stay. They might need a woman for some reason, and my status could pose a problem." She gave Sherrie a look. "And besides, if I leave you here, poor Chris won't get any work done."

Leroux's cheeks burned and his heart ached as Tong turned back toward her keyboard, her torch for him apparently still not extinguished.

Sherrie gave him another kiss for the ages. "You're probably right. Now, back to business. Do they have a destination yet?"

Tommy nodded then turned back to face his keyboard. "Check out this footage." He tapped several keys then turned back and indicated the large display. The camera angle at the airport raced forward, showing a private jet landing, its door opening, the stairs extending, then two men with Maggie between them disembarking. They walked across the tarmac to a waiting helicopter and it lifted off immediately.

Leroux cursed. "That widens the search area. Please tell me you know where they went."

Tommy twisted in his chair and tapped a few keys. A map of the region appeared, showing scores of icons depicting every plane and helicopter in the sky. One was highlighted in red. "That's the helicopter there." He tapped a key several times and the air traffic display jumped ahead, showing the red indicator stationary in New York City.

"You have the address?"

"Yup."

"Send it to the team. And get me everything you can on that building. Images, video, layouts, occupants. I want to know everything we can if they're going to hit it."

"You got it, boss."

Leroux turned to Tong. "Any luck tracing that holding company?"

"Nothing tracing back to the mob yet. Almost everything is in a legal firm's name, but I'm making progress. But I'll tell you one thing"—Tong jutted her chin toward the now zoomed-in display, the address now shown—"that address is owned by one of the shell corporations. I recognize it from a list of real estate holdings I looked at just a few minutes ago."

Leroux pursed his lips as he stared at the screen. "If they own it, then that means they could have customized the shit out of every floor."

"Twelve floors," tossed Tommy over his shoulder.

"All twelve floors will likely be hostile," said Fang. "We need to figure out where she is in that building if they're going to have any chance."

126

Sherrie folded her arms and stared at the screen, her lips pursed. "The Agency has a little toy that might just help with that, but I don't know how we're going to get our hands on it."

Leroux grunted. "From what I've seen, Dylan can get his hands on pretty much anything."

"I'm not so sure if even his people can get this."

CIA Headquarters

Langley, Virginia

Morrison couldn't remember the last time he had been in this particular sub-basement level of CIA headquarters. It had been years, perhaps even a decade, and the young woman behind the counter was certainly shocked to see someone of his rank standing at her counter like any other operative seeking equipment.

"Chief, I don't think I've ever seen you down here."

"And you didn't see me today."

Her eyes bulged. "Sir?"

He slipped her a piece of paper and her eyebrows shot up her forehead as she read it.

"You want these?"

"Yes. Off the books."

She lowered her voice. "Off the books?"

"Yes."

She checked over both shoulders, confirming they were alone. "For how long?"

"If all goes well, less than twenty-four hours."

She gulped. "I can lose my job for this. What if they decide to do a random inspection during those twenty-four hours and find them missing from the inventory?"

"Then you'll be calling me, and then I'll be making a call, and then the inventory will be corrected."

Her shoulders slumped. "Give me a moment." She placed her hand on a palm scanner and a heavy metal door opened. She stepped inside and closed the door as Morrison fished a cigarette lighter that he always carried with him out of his pocket, not because he smoked, but because it was a cherished gift from President Reagan when he had helped save his life years ago at the beginning of his career.

And it was also handy in situations like this.

He picked up the piece of paper still lying on the counter and flicked the lighter, the flame reliably appearing. He lit the corner of the page then returned the lighter to his pocket as the flame quickly engulfed the specially coated paper, a ream of which he kept in a locked drawer in his office. Within seconds, the paper was no more.

The door opened and the supply officer stepped back into the room, holding a case about the size of a box of cigars. She slid it across the counter. "Twelve micro-drones with laser-enhanced listening capabilities, and one master controller interface."

Morrison reached out to take the box, but the woman didn't let go.

"Twenty-four hours?"

"Perhaps less."

She let go. He turned for the door when she stopped him. "Sir, tomorrow I work the graveyard shift. Midnight until eight AM. Whatever you do, don't bring it back before that."

Morrison acknowledged the instructions then headed for the parking garage, the box held under his arm. He turned the corner to see a waving Sherrie with a broad smile.

"Working late tonight, Chief?"

"My sister-in-law is visiting."

Sherrie laughed. "Let me guess, she's not your biggest fan."

He grunted. "That's one way of putting it. What are you doing here? I thought I gave you the weekend off."

"I forgot something in my locker. Something sexy." She held up a bag. "You want to see?"

Morrison held up a hand, stopping her. "A man my age shouldn't put his heart at risk."

She giggled. "You're so sweet."

He gestured toward his car. "This is me." He unlocked it with the fob then climbed inside. "Where are you parked?"

"Not far. Have a good night, Chief."

"You too."

She walked away and he backed out of the spot, the car's lights illuminating her athletic figure. She was a stunning woman, and he couldn't help but form a mental image of her in whatever shockingly skimpy outfit that might be in that bag. He shook his head.

You dirty old bastard.

This was all Leroux's idea for the sake of the cameras. For all he knew, it was a sweatshirt in that bag, though he had no doubt she could make even that sexy.

She stumbled but regained her balance and took a ginger step, wincing. She leaned against a nearby support post as he pulled up beside her and rolled down the passenger window.

"Are you okay?"

"I think I twisted my ankle a bit."

He unlocked the doors and removed the box of misappropriated gear from the seat. "Get in. I'll drive you to your car."

She smiled and climbed in, closing the door. She put the bag down between her legs and he handed her the box. He slowly advanced, and as they crossed in front of the pillar, she slipped the box into the bag then leaned forward and massaged her ankle as the camera dead-zone ended. "I think it's going to be fine." She sat back up and pointed ahead. "That's my car there." He came to a halt behind it and she opened her door, swinging her leg out. She circled her foot several times and smiled. "Yeah, it's fine now. Thanks so much, Chief." She climbed out with her bag then closed the door.

"You have a good night now."

"You too."

He pulled away, his heart hammering. He rarely got to do anything tradecraft related, and this was exciting despite the fact it could end his career if he were caught. He sighed as he pulled out of the lot. If he had to go out helping save an innocent woman, he'd have no regrets.

Though he'd never hear the end of it if his sister-in-law found out.

West 6th Street

New York City, New York

Dawson leaned over and stared at the contents of the small box Sherrie had just brought from Langley. The team was split between two SUVs parked several blocks north of the target building, and their entire plan was predicated upon knowing where Maggie was in the 12-story structure. Kane was convinced the box's contents were key to their success, but now that Dawson had seen it, he was skeptical.

Niner voiced everyone's concerns. "What the hell are those?"

Kane reached in and retrieved a small case, barely the size of a silver dollar. He snapped it open, revealing an even smaller device inside.

Atlas' voice rumbled from the back row. "Is that a drone?"

"Yup. One of the most sophisticated drones out there." Kane held it in the palm of his hand. "Obviously it's tiny, so it's hard to spot, but they're designed to work as a hive. We deploy them all, give them the target, and they'll map all the windows then attach themselves in sequence. They use a laser to monitor the vibrations on the glass so we can hear what's happening on the other side."

He tapped a USB stick in the box. "We control everything with this. As we clear each room, we can send the drone off to another room. We can cover that entire building very quickly, and hopefully by the time we're done, we'll know where Maggie is."

Dawson was still skeptical. "Have you ever used these before?"

Kane shook his head. "Nope, this will be the first time. I've wanted to try them out since I heard about them. They're bleeding edge experimental."

Atlas grunted. "Let's hope not temperamental too."

Sherrie stabbed a finger at Kane. "And remember, be careful with those. Only the Chief knows we have them, and he stuck his neck out to get them. We're supposed to have them back in his hands in less than twenty-four hours, otherwise the shit's going to hit the fan."

Niner leaned back in his seat, holding his hands up. "I'm not touching the little guys. I'm afraid I'd break them."

Atlas eyed him. "With those dainty little fingers? Not likely."

Niner motioned toward Atlas' meaty paws. "I'd rather have dainty hands than those Comic-Con novelty fists."

Atlas held up his hands, examining them. "They're proportional."

Niner rolled his eyes. "This is why you have to go through everything sideways." He leaned closer to his friend's hands. "How do you even get something out of the microwave with those things? Do you have to use tongs?"

Atlas clenched his fists. "I just shake one of these and make you my bitch, then you fetch me whatever I want."

Everyone roared and Niner held his own fists up to Atlas'. "My God, I think they're four times the size."

"That's not all that's—"

Dawson raised a finger, cutting him off. "We have a lady present."

Kane guffawed. "I've worked with her. Trust me, she's no lady."

Sherrie grinned at him. "Why, thank you."

Kane plugged the drone interface into his laptop and configured the experimental devices. He uploaded the coordinates for the building, a map appearing showing their position and the planned route to the target.

Niner turned to Sherrie as they waited. "Are you coming in with us?"

She shrugged and addressed Kane. "I don't know. Am I?"

Kane shook his head and continued to work. "No, you and I will be monitoring things from here."

Atlas frowned. "That's too bad. It would have been nice to have someone who watched my back rather than my ass."

Niner eyed him. "Is that comment directed at me?"

Atlas shrugged. "No. Interesting though that you assumed it was."

"With an ass as big as yours, it's hard not to. It kind of occupies half my field of vision when it crosses in front of me."

Atlas gave him a look. "I'll have you know I'm less than four-percent body fat."

"Well, if there's another guy out there your size with the other ninety-six, it might explain America's obesity statistics."

Sherrie stared at him. "Huh?"

Niner shrugged. "I don't know, even I can't explain that one. It came out wrong."

Atlas grunted. "They can't all be gems. It'd be nice if at least a few of them were, though."

Niner flipped him the bird. "I'm hilarious and you know it. You can only dream of being as funny as me. I have Vanessa in stitches every time I'm over."

"She's just being polite. I think she actually finds you quite tiresome."

"I think you're just jealous that I can make her laugh and you can't."

Kane cleared his throat. "If you juveniles are done, we're ready to go."

"So, what do we do now?" asked Dawson.

"That all depends."

"On what?"

"Are you ready to go?"

"Yup."

Kane rolled down the window and clicked a button on the laptop. The micro-drones lifted from the dash and flew out the window, disappearing into the night sky. On the screen, the map updated, red dots indicating the positions of each device.

Niner leaned forward. "What? No video?"

Kane shook his head. "That's not what these are designed for. These are for listening, and video just chews up power and space. I understand the next generation, however, might have both capabilities."

"Cool. Call me when you get some. I'm convinced my neighbors are talking about me."

Jagger eyed him. "You don't just need audio?"

"Did I mention the neighbors are cute?"

Atlas punched him on the shoulder. "Cuter than Angela?"

Niner's eyes flared momentarily as he rubbed his arm. "Man, I'm really not used to having a girlfriend, am I?"

"Apparently not."

"The drones have reached the target building," said Kane. The image on the screen changed, a wire diagram appearing with the external architecture displayed, including the windows. One of the windows flashed, more following.

"What's that?" asked Dawson.

"The drones are attaching to the windows and recording the audio. Each will listen for sixty seconds, and if it doesn't hear anything, move on to the next assigned window. If it does hear something, it will flag it and put it into the queue for us to review."

Niner leaned back. "This could take a while."

"It could. There are a lot of windows, but remember the time of night. Hopefully there are not too many people there."

Sherrie pointed at the laptop she held. "We've got something in the queue."

Kane handed her a pair of headphones and she jacked into the laptop. She brought up the file and listened.

"Two Russians, male, talking about a football game, Spartak versus Dynamo." She continued to listen and shook her head. "Nothing of interest here." Another file popped up on the screen and she clicked on it. "Sounds like a group, at least three or more." Her eyes widened. "Hey, they're talking about you guys. One of them is saying that the only way their team was taken out so easily was if Special Forces were involved."

"They got that right," agreed Niner. Atlas fist-bumped him.

"Any indication they're expecting us?" asked Dawson.

Sherrie shook her head. "No, I'm hearing a lot of glasses clinking on tables. I'm guessing they're into the vodka. One of them is now telling a story about the first mission he went on with one of the dead. Nobody's mentioned Maggie." She brought up another file and gasped.

Dawson leaned forward. "What is it?"

Sherrie's eyes glistened as she turned toward him. "I don't think you want to hear this."

Dawson tensed, his stomach churning. "Play it."

She unplugged the headphones and replayed the recording. There was a loud noise, then a woman cried out in agony. "Please, I've told you everything!" Another loud noise and more pleading and sobbing. "Why are you doing this?" she cried. Dawson closed his eyes as his fists clenched. There was no doubt it was Maggie. And there was no doubt they were beating her. Another blow and Maggie screamed, "Why don't you ask me any questions?" The recording cut off, the 60 seconds finished.

Dawson opened his eyes and Kane pointed at a highlighted window. "She's in this room. Seventh floor."

Dawson cursed. "Six floors from the roof, seven to the ground."

Niner brought up an aerial view on his tablet. "Look at this. These buildings are packed together like sardines. There's maybe twenty feet between the target and the building to the north. And it's only a few stories taller. I say we get to the top of this building, fire a line over, slide down like James Bond, then rappel to the seventh floor. We retrieve Maggie, rappel down the rest of the way. We could be in and out in a couple of minutes."

Dawson's head slowly bobbed as he stared at the flashing window. "It sounds like as good a plan as any." He pointed at the laptop. "Let's get those drones concentrated around that room. I want to know what else we might be facing."

"You got it," said Kane, going to work.

Dawson activated his comms. "Zero-Two, Zero-One. We found her."

AG Office Suites Tower, West 6ᵗʰ Street

New York City, New York

Chuck sat behind the security desk, barely awake. If you had asked him a few years ago, he would have said this was his dream job—the night shift. Nobody to deal with beyond the occasional worker burning the midnight oil, and a boss who called in at the beginning and end of the shift, too lazy to do the proper checks he was supposed to. Chuck's job was to sign everyone in and out, monitor the alarm panel, and call the police or fire if anything showed up. In the two years he had worked here, not once had any light on that panel shown anything. It was a perfect, boring job, with little to no responsibility, and no one harping at him.

And he hated it.

He hadn't always hated it. When he had started, he hadn't realized how much his mind desperately craved stimulation. He was an avid reader, graphic novels his preferred choice, but it had been made crystal clear to him when he was hired that he too was on camera and monitored, and wasn't to be distracted. That meant no reading, no surfing the Internet, nothing to occupy his time but stare at the monitors that showed the corridors and stairs he was responsible for.

He'd love to quit, but his parents had read him the riot act. If he wanted to continue living at home, he had to either have a full-time job or go to college. There was no other option. He had no idea what to do with his life. His grades had never been great, so he had taken what he assumed would be the easier option—get a job. And he was beginning to think he had made the wrong choice.

As soon as he had grumbled about it at the dinner table one night, he came home the next day to find over a dozen brochures for various colleges in the area. What had surprised him was that he was actually considering applying for the winter session, though if he did, it meant four more years of living at home, and he had finally saved enough money to get his own place. And independence sounded wonderful. But it also meant staying in this depressing job.

An indicator beeped and he checked the display, one of the monitors automatically switching to the main doors. What it showed had his blood running cold, and if he hadn't just gone to the bathroom, he would have soiled himself. Half a dozen masked men were entering the building, heavily armed, all dressed as if they had just walked off the set of a Call of Duty production. He continued to stare at the screen, his mouth agape, when someone cleared their throat directly in front of him.

His head jerked up as he realized the camera he was watching was the lobby camera. A hulking Black man and a small Asian man, if the eyes revealed by the mask weren't lying, stood in front of him, the former scowling at him, the latter smiling pleasantly as the other men continued toward the elevators.

"Sorry to interrupt your evening, but we're going to need to borrow your roof for a few minutes. Any objections?"

The Black man growled and Chuck shook his head rapidly.

The Asian's smile broadened. "Excellent. Do you have the keys or whatever is required to access the roof?"

Chuck nodded.

"Good, then follow us."

Chuck hesitated. There was a panic button underneath the desk directly in front of him. Press it and they would never know.

The bulging Black man leaned forward. "We really must insist." He leaned even closer. "And if you press the silent alarm, we'll know, and it won't end well for you"

Chuck's bladder discovered it wasn't completely empty. He rose, his knees shaking, and rounded the desk, hoping the fact his pants were black would hide his shame. The Asian glanced down and frowned.

"I'm sorry about that. We didn't mean to scare you, but my friend's not in a good mood. He just heard they recast the new Hulk and he never got a call to audition." They boarded the elevator with the other men and the Asian indicated the panel. "I'll let you drive."

Chuck swept his pass and pressed the button for the top floor. As they rode up, no one said anything, but all around him the sounds of gear being checked and weapons readied had his heart hammering faster than he could ever remember it doing. He was going to die. He had no doubt these men weren't police. All they would have to do was show a badge and they would have his complete cooperation. These were criminals.

Or terrorists.

And why did they want to get on the roof? It made no sense to him. There was nothing important up there. Nothing of value. His heart nearly stopped with a thought. From the roof, they would have clear views of several blocks of the city. They could shoot scores of pedestrians.

But only if they could get on the roof.

He had always wanted to do something with his life. Well, that wasn't entirely true. As of late, he had begun to think he should be doing something with his life. Perhaps dying here, right now, saving potentially dozens of lives, could be that something.

He sucked in a deep breath, hoping it would bring him some courage, but it didn't. "Why do you need to get on the roof?"

The Asian smiled. "That's none of your concern."

Chuck closed his eyes, clenching his fists. "It is if you're going to kill people."

"What makes you think we're going to kill people?"

Chuck opened his eyes, staring at the elevator doors, the brushed metal revealing only the shadows of those surrounding him. "Are you serious? Have you seen yourselves?"

The Asian chuckled. "You're right. We are going to kill people, but they're bad people."

Chuck gulped. "Bad in your opinion, or actually bad?"

A woman's screams filled the elevator, the sounds of her begging for mercy punctuated by what he had no doubt were vicious blows. The recording cut off.

A new voice spoke behind him. "The people we're going to kill are doing that to her. They're Russian mob. Any more questions?"

Chuck's eyes bulged. Russian mob. Suddenly it all made sense. He had heard some rumors about the building next to theirs, rumors he had dismissed as his fellow security guards merely scaring the new guy. Perhaps they had been true after all. There was no doubt the recording that had just been played was of a woman being beaten. Viscously beaten. He still had no idea who these men were, but if they were willing to take on the Russian mob in an effort to save some woman from being tortured, they wouldn't hesitate to kill him. He would die for nothing, because no one would call him a hero if all he did was save the lives of Russian criminals.

He turned. "Who is she to you?"

The man didn't answer, but the pain in his eyes told Chuck everything he needed to know. She was important to him.

The elevator chimed and the doors opened.

"What can I do to help?"

The Asian slapped him on the back. "I knew you'd come around. All we need you to do is get us on the roof. We'll do the rest."

Chuck led them up a stairwell. He swiped his pass and entered a code, opening the rooftop access door. The heavily armed men filed past him as he pressed his back against the wall, holding the door open.

The Asian smiled at him. "Thank you for your cooperation."

"What do I do now?"

"Return to your post."

"That's it? You're not worried that I might call the police?"

The man laughed. "Buddy, the police are going to be called in the next few minutes regardless. In fact, just so you don't get into any trouble, go back to your post and call in what just happened. Tell them we forced you to let us on the roof."

Chuck nodded and the man disappeared through the door. He remained pressed against the wall as he struggled to calm his racing heart. He closed his eyes in an attempt to steady his nerves, but all that did was free up his mind to remember the screams of the poor woman. If these men were telling the truth, that they were on a rescue mission to save this woman from the Russian mob, then all he could do was wish them well.

He opened his eyes and headed back down the stairs, taking his time. He would make the call as instructed, but he wasn't going to be in a rush about it. He just wished he knew what was going on.

Gunfire erupted overhead and he yelped then sprinted down the remaining steps.

There were other places farther from the action where he could take his time.

Suspected Russian Mob Stronghold, West 6th Street

New York City, New York

Dawson cursed. Everything had been going perfectly. They had accessed the rooftop without incident. Red's team was stationed outside operating a drone with a view of the roof, and had radioed in the all-clear. Atlas had hurled a rope with a grappling hook, the prongs gripping on the first try. Niner had slid across first, followed by Atlas then their gear. Dawson had come across last, and that was when their carefully laid plans went awry.

The rooftop door on their target building opened, four men stepping out, laughing boisterously, one already with a joint between his lips, a lighter sparking in the dark.

They had no time to waste. They couldn't simply hide and wait out these men. Maggie was being assaulted, and every moment prolonged her suffering. He rose from his position behind a large HVAC system, his suppressed Glock belching lead. Two dropped before the others even reacted. Atlas took out the third, but the fourth fell back through the doorway, and a moment later he shouted a warning in Russian followed by the rattle of an Uzi, its muzzle flashes framed by the darkened stairwell.

The hostile was firing blindly, and Dawson indicated for Niner and Atlas to advance. The two men rushed forward, careful to stay out of the line of fire, both reaching the wall framing the door. The gunfire stopped momentarily as the Russian reloaded, and Atlas stepped in front of the door, his MP5 at the ready, and squeezed out two bursts.

"Clear!" he announced.

Dawson pointed at the gear. "Start rigging everything. Our element of surprise is blown."

Mickey and Jagger quickly went to work as Atlas and Niner held their positions at the door. Niner cursed. "Hey, BD, it sounds like they're going apeshit down there. What do you want us to do?"

"Rig the door. After the first few get toasted, the rest might think twice."

"Roger that."

Atlas covered Niner as he wired the door with a little surprise.

Dawson activated his comms, shaking his head at Kane's callsign. "Chunky-Monkey, Zero-One. Status report."

Kane immediately replied. "I think I outdid myself on that callsign. They're going apeshit for sure. We're picking up dozens of voices."

"Is Maggie still in the target room?"

"As far as we can tell, yes, but Sherrie just heard someone say, 'Get the girl.'"

Dawson cursed as he strode toward the ropes Mickey and Jagger were working on. Jagger read his intent and pointed at one of them.

"That one's ready."

Dawson grabbed it and clipped himself on then dropped over the edge, rapidly descending toward the seventh floor, mentally counting the windows.

Red's voice chirped in his ear. "Zero-One, Zero-Two. Two more floors. Over."

Dawson slowed his descent, coming to a halt just above the seventh floor. He twisted 90 degrees so he was parallel to the window frame, then tore open the Velcro of one of his many pockets. He fished out a small charge then reached down and placed it on the glass as the rest of the team sprinted down the side of the building, tightening their brakes as they neared him.

Dawson held up three fingers then counted down silently before turning his body, triggering the small device. The window shattered below him and he released the brake, rapidly dropping five feet as his Glock swept from left to right. He fired two rounds, dropping the first hostile, his aim already switching to the next as two of his men joined him in the now glassless window. More gunfire erupted from the others and the enemy continued to drop, everyone carefully avoiding the high-backed chair that could only hold Maggie.

"Clear!" shouted Mickey, Jagger confirming.

Dawson unbuckled and stepped inside, cautiously advancing as the others did the same. He rounded the back of the chair, bracing for what would truly be a horrific sight. And what he saw he could never have prepared himself for.

The chair was empty.

Dawson activated his comms as Atlas and Niner swung into the room. "Chunky-Monkey, Zero-One. She's not here! Report!"

"Sorry, Zero-One. It sounded like two men entered the room just before you blew the glass. One of them said, 'the boss said to get her to the roof.' Once you blew the glass, we couldn't hear anything. They must have got her out just as you were coming in."

Dawson headed for the door as Niner asked the question that demanded an answer. "Why the hell would they take her to the roof?"

And Atlas' answer sent a chill down Dawson's spine. "Maybe they intend to take her on that shiny black helicopter that was sitting up there."

Niner cursed. "Oh my God! We rigged the door. If she…"

Dawson yanked open the door and poked his head out, finding the hallway clear, the only woman he had ever loved nowhere in sight.

"They're not going to make it!" cried Sherrie as everyone else realized what Niner already had.

Kane cursed as the feed from the drone observing the rooftop showed the helicopter powering up, its massive rotors beginning to turn. He repositioned the drone so he could see the door Maggie could be coming through at any moment. He zoomed in then activated his comms. "One-One, confirm you just used a trip wire detonator on that door."

"Confirmed," replied Niner. "Door opens, trips the wire. Kaboom!"

"Copy that."

"What are you planning?" asked Sherrie.

Kane frowned as he guided the drone. "Sweetheart, Hail Marys are never planned."

The drone sped toward the door, the explosive growing in the camera frame, then abruptly the image went dark, the signal broken as the sky one block away flashed, flame lighting the night briefly. He jerked a thumb over his shoulder. "Deploy the backup drone."

Sherrie leaped over the seats and unzipped one of the duffel bags as Kane answered Dawson's, "What the hell was that?" call.

"I used the roof drone to detonate the explosive."

"Why the hell did you do that? You could have killed her!"

"If they opened that door, she was dead anyway. But if they didn't reach it yet, she'll be fine. Depending on the damage, it might just keep her in the building."

A string of colorful metaphors burst through Kane's earpiece before Dawson finally replied. "Good thinking. Deploy the backup drone. We need eyes on that rooftop."

"Way ahead of you, buddy."

Dawson sprinted down the corridor, the team on his heels. He reached the doors for the stairwell then held up a fist, bringing everyone to a halt. He pressed his ear against the cool metal door, the pounding of footsteps revealed, several men shouting in Russian. He peered through the small pane of glass then jerked back as two men rushed past, heading down.

"Where the hell are we supposed to go?" asked one of them in Russian.

"Who the hell cares? We just need to get out of here. The police are going to be here any minute."

"What about the boss?"

"He's taking the helicopter. He's probably already gone."

The other cursed. "It's good to be the king."

Dawson cautiously opened the door then peered over the railing, spotting at least half a dozen people evacuating below, with more footfalls echoing above them. He gripped his weapon tighter.

Looks like we're killing our way to the top.

Which suited him just fine.

Maggie lay in the stairwell, dazed and confused, though only partially from the explosion that had just ripped apart the floor above them. Debris was scattered everywhere, and she might have been concerned that if the blast had gone off just five seconds later, she'd be dead. Yet that's what she wanted. Death. The sweet release from her pain. She could barely see, her eyes nearly swollen shut. Her lip was cracked and she could taste blood in her mouth. Her chest and stomach were in agony from the blows that had rained down upon her when they had first taken her from the parking lot, and when they arrived at the motel, she feared her captors were planning to rape her. Instead, they had laid a beating on her, forcing her to give up the names of her friends as well as her Facebook password so they could get pictures of them.

She was ashamed of how quickly they had broken her. She had watched countless movies depicting torture scenes where the victim held out, and she was certain her fiancé had been tortured during his career. She could never imagine him giving in. He was too strong. But the unrelenting pain, the terror, had proven too much too quickly, and within minutes she was telling them anything they wanted to hear, then had sobbed, having served up her friends' lives merely to stop the pain.

Part of her had prayed for death once they had what they wanted from her, so she wouldn't have to live with the shame and guilt, but that wasn't to be. Something had gone wrong, and she and the two men that had captured her were soon on an airplane, then a helicopter, before she was shown to a room in what appeared to be an office building.

Then the beatings had resumed in earnest, with the questions focusing on who had killed their men. But this time she had something believable to tell them. She didn't know. Though in reality, she did. If police were responsible, then the question wouldn't be asked. The fact they didn't know, meant it was somebody unexpected, and that had to be her beloved and the other team members.

And the fact this building was now under attack told her they were still fighting to save her.

Her entire body ached, and the blast that had thrown her against the wall and showered her in debris had delivered more bruises, though as far as she could tell, no new broken bones. She didn't hear any gunfire overhead, though it echoed below them, and it didn't make sense. If they were blowing the door, they had obviously succeeded, so why weren't they coming in?

She was hauled to her feet, one of her captors holding her by the throat as the other gingerly made his way up the stairwell. He disappeared from sight then a moment later shouted something in Russian. She was hauled up the stairs and through the twisted mess of a doorway at the top. Most of the wall was caved in, the source of the debris scattered about, yet again, she heard no gunfire, no challenge from Dawson or his team.

Only the thunder of a helicopter.

Footfalls pounded below them and both men spun, aiming their weapons down the stairs they had just climbed. The man in charge appeared and one of her captors opened fire, unfortunately missing the bastard. What she had to assume were curses were shouted from below and both weapons were raised with apologies made. The man in charge reappeared and was helped through the debris and out onto the roof.

They hurried to the helicopter and climbed on board, lifting off moments later. As they rose, she spotted a drone rapidly approaching, and she pressed her face against the window so there could be no doubt she was on board. Someone yanked her hair, throwing her onto the floor as the pilot asked something.

And her heart sank when the boss replied.

"Moskva."

Sherrie pointed at the screen. "There she is!"

Kane cursed at the sight of Maggie's face against the glass, and his heart ached at the visual evidence of the brutal beating they had heard. Suddenly she disappeared, someone having noticed what she was doing. He activated his comms. "Zero-One, Chunky-Monkey. Chopper has cleared the roof with Maggie on board, over."

Dawson replied, the thunder of gunfire periodically overwhelming the audio. "This is Zero-One. Can you confirm she's absolutely on board?"

"Affirmative, Zero-One. We have a clear shot of her on board, over."

"Then track it. We need to know where the hell they're going."

Sherrie gave a thumbs-up, already talking to Leroux.

"We're already on it. Recommend you make a rapid egress before local authorities arrive."

"Copy that. Zero-One, out."

Kane switched channels to hear Leroux.

"Looks like they're heading back to the private airport," said his best friend. "I'm going to try and see if we can find a flight plan."

"Do what you can. BD's going to want a destination for his rage."

"Copy that. I'll get back to you as soon as we have something. Control, out."

Sherrie flinched as gunfire erupted down the street.

"Oh shit," muttered Kane.

"What?"

"I think we're about to make the national news."

Red peered from his position across the street as several people emerged from the target building, one of them carrying a weapon. He activated his comms. "Zero-One, Zero-Two. We've got hostiles emerging. What do you want us to do, over?"

"If they've got a weapon, take them out," came Dawson's curt reply.

Red smiled. "Roger that."

He took aim and squeezed the trigger, dropping the armed man. The other two, unarmed, scrambled in opposite directions and he let them go. Two more emerged, but this time they sprayed the area blindly with automatic weapons fire. Red dropped one of them as someone else on the team took out the other. This was too easy, and for a moment he felt guilty before reminding himself just who these people were.

Russian mob.

They committed unspeakable crimes on a daily basis, but more importantly, they had killed Joanne, wounded Vanessa, and kidnapped then tortured Maggie. Not to mention they had scared the living shit out of his wife.

Every damned one of them should die as far as he was concerned, but he agreed with Dawson's orders—only if they had a weapon.

Wings' voice came in over the comm. "Zero-Two, One-Two. I've got a bunch of them coming out a side emergency exit. Looks like they're using some women as human shields, over."

Red cursed. "Only take the shot if it's clean," he replied. "Those women are probably victims of human trafficking. They're innocent in this."

"Roger that, Zero-Two. Engaging now."

Gunfire, slightly to his left, rattled through the alley as two women emerged from the front entrance of the building, their hands up as they crouched.

"Hold your fire!" shouted Red, and the two women ran off together as sirens wailed in the distance. "Zero-One, Zero-Two. Locals are about to arrive. We need to get out of here now."

"Copy that, Zero-Two, we're a little busy here."

"Perimeter team, Zero-Two. Be prepared to evac at the first visual on the locals, over."

A string of acknowledgments were received as Red repositioned to cover both the front door and the alley where Wings had engaged. A man emerged from the alleyway, a scantily-clad woman held tightly against him, his eyes wide with panic as his head spun side to side. Red took aim and squeezed the trigger once, the bullet creating a new unnecessary hole in the man's head. He collapsed in a heap and the woman screamed. Red waved a hand at her, indicating she should get the hell out of there. She did.

He advanced across the street, the front door no longer popular among their targets, but the alleyway filled with gunfire and the screams of the helpless.

Hurry up, BD, before our luck runs out.

Dawson slung his MP5 then drew his Glock as they continued to advance down the stairwell. They had no way of knowing how many people were in the building, but he had personally taken out at least a dozen, and would be content to spend the rest of the night clearing the building of the vermin that infested it.

Unfortunately, he had made a promise to the colonel that he wouldn't make the evening news.

A woman poked her head out from a door on the next landing and he held his fire. Her eyes bulged at the sight of them and she ducked back behind the door. But something wasn't right. He could have sworn he heard a weapon being checked, and he wasn't about to leave that potential threat behind them. He indicated for his men to remain quiet as they filed past. Dawson took a position at the bottom of the next landing with a clear shot as the others continued. The door opened slightly and the woman emerged, a pistol gripped in her hands. Dawson placed two in her chest.

I guess assuming all the bad guys are guys is sexist.

Her motionless body held the door open and he rose, confirming no one else was with her, then followed his team, covering their rear as they rushed down the steps.

"Zero-One, Zero-Two. We've got flashing lights."

"Copy that, Zero-Two." Dawson checked the number on the door he had just passed. "We're on the second floor. Meet you at the rendezvous point."

"Copy that."

Two shots from a Glock pounded the confined space as Niner took out another hostile. Dawson stepped over the corpse and checked the door before continuing after his men, and moments later was in the lobby. They sprinted across the marble floor and emerged through the doors and into the night. A horn honked as Kane pulled up in their SUV and everyone piled inside. Kane floored it, then took the first right, easing off the gas so as not to stand out as a police car sped past. He continued for a couple of blocks then pulled to the side of the road and rolled down his window. A moment later the micro-drones flew inside and came to rest on the dash where they had taken off from.

"Do we have time for this?" asked Dawson, frustrated.

"If you ever want the Chief to help us in the future, then we make the time."

"That's twelve," said Sherrie as she returned them to their cases.

Kane hit the gas as Dawson activated his comms. "Zero-Two, Zero-One. Status, over."

"We're clear, Zero-One. Heading for the rendezvous point."

"Copy that." Dawson turned his attention to Sherrie, letting Kane focus on driving. "Any word on that chopper?"

"It's heading directly for the same private airport where the plane landed."

Dawson cursed. "If they get her on that plane, we're never going to see her again."

Sherrie reached out and squeezed his hand. "You're forgetting one thing."

"What's that?"

"As soon as they leave American soil, the CIA can get involved, which opens up a whole bunch of possibilities."

She was right, though the thought of Maggie being taken to a foreign country still overwhelmed him with fear for her safety. He smashed his fist on Kane's seatback. "We should have taken out the chopper when we first hit the roof."

Atlas leaned forward from the rear row. "We were trying for the element of surprise. Let's save the second-guessing for the mission debrief."

Niner groaned. "Oh man. Mission debrief? I thought this was off the books. You're telling me I'm going to have to do paperwork? If I had known we were following protocols, I would have kept count of how many I killed." He eyed Atlas. "How many did you kill?"

"Five."

"Okay, then I must have killed six."

"And if I had said six?"

Niner grinned. "You know the answer to that."

Off-the-books Operations Center

Outside Bethesda, Maryland

Tong whistled as she leaned back from her station.

"What is it?" asked Leroux.

"They just filed a flight plan."

Everyone in the room turned.

"Destination?"

"Moscow."

Tommy inhaled a quick breath. "She's dead."

Fang regarding him. "What makes you think that?"

Tommy shrugged. "Well, they're going home, aren't they? I mean, they're heading back to Russia so that we can't touch them, and she's a loose end."

Leroux folded his arms, leaning back in his chair. "If they take her on the plane, then she'll most likely be alive when they land in Moscow. There's no point in transporting someone you intend to kill." He sensed Tong had something else to say as her fingers drummed on the workstation. "That whistle of yours, I think, suggested something a little bit bigger than just Moscow being the destination."

She smiled at him. "You know me so well."

"That's why we work so well together. What did you find?"

She tapped the monitor. "The flight just got diplomatic status."

Leroux's jaw dropped. "Are you serious?"

"Yup. The Russian Embassy just registered it as a diplomatic flight."

"What does that mean?" asked Tommy.

"It means we can't touch it," replied Tong.

Leroux stared at the display. "More importantly, it means that these people are extremely well connected within the Russian government." He stabbed a finger at the display. "We need to find out who issued that. It has to be somebody with a lot of pull to be able to do it last-minute. There is no way that flight was planned for." Tong leaned forward, her fingers already at work as Leroux reached for his headset. "I better tell Dylan and BD. They are *not* going to be happy."

Highlawn Avenue

New York City, New York

Dawson and the others stripped out of their gear, the parking garage they were in hiding them from prying eyes. Leroux and his team had already overridden the cameras, so there would be no video of them arriving or leaving. Kane's contacts had already delivered two fresh vehicles and would be retrieving the two used in the attack, along with all the equipment, then sanitizing everything before the hour was out. There would be no evidence of their involvement, nothing left to trace back to them.

Nobody said anything as they donned civilian attire then piled into their new vehicles. Dawson let Niner drive as they snaked out of the garage and into the night. Sitting in the middle row, Atlas handed out new comms from a care package Kane's people had left in the back.

Dawson activated his. "Chunky-Monkey, Zero-One. Status?"

Kane, who had gone on ahead with Sherrie to set up their gear, replied immediately. "I've got a name that you probably won't recognize, but when I tell you who it is, you're not going to be happy."

Dawson bristled. "Give it to me."

"The plane was given diplomatic status by Mikhail Novak. He's the Minister of Energy in the Russian government. Staunch ally of the President. But get this, he's a law-and-order guy. Constantly speaking out against gang activity."

Niner glanced over at Dawson for a moment. "Why the hell would a tough-on-crime Russian minister arrange a getaway flight for Russian mobsters?"

Dawson shrugged. "Does he make a habit out of this?" he asked, reactivating his comms.

"We don't know yet," replied Kane. "I had a hell of a time getting this info outside of regular channels. I've got my contacts pulling all diplomatic flight requests approved by him. I'll hopefully have an answer shortly, but regardless of what we find, this takes things to an entirely new level."

Dawson gripped his seat belt. The moment he had heard the flight's destination, there was no doubt everything had changed. It was one thing to go off the reservation and go all vigilante on Russian mob ass on home soil, it was a completely different thing to do the same in Moscow. Yet if that's where Maggie was being taken, he had no choice but to follow.

"Buddy, I need to know if you intend to go to Moscow."

Dawson didn't hesitate. "I do. I'm not stopping until I have Maggie back, and if I can't get her back, then I'm going to kill every last one of them."

"Hear hear!" cried Niner, punching the steering wheel twice with the palm of his fist. "Count me in!"

"Me too," was echoed from the others in the back.

Kane's sigh caused a burst of static. "I was afraid you were going to say that. There's no way in hell I can get all of you in."

Dawson grunted. "I had no idea you could get even one of us in."

"Buddy, I can guarantee you if you fly in commercial, you'll be flagged the moment you step off the plane. I think we have to take a page from our Russian friends, but you're going to have to pare down the team. Six people. That's it."

"Understood."

Four volunteers indicated their desire to go before Dawson could say anything else.

Atlas chuckled. "Everyone who chose to get in Red's car chose poorly."

Niner shrugged. "There's still one slot available. Maybe they can draw straws."

Dawson shook his head. "No, the sixth position goes to Spock. He deserves the kill."

Heads bobbed in agreement, Niner giving a thumbs-up. "Good choice. Let's get our asses to Moscow, get Maggie back, and pound a lot of Russian ass."

Everyone snickered and Atlas reached forward, shaking Niner's shoulder. "You go ahead and pound all the ass you want over there. We'll just kill them after you're done."

Niner eyed him in the rearview mirror. "What the hell are you talking about?"

"Think about it, buddy. Think about it."

Niner squinted as he replayed the conversation.

Then pounded his head against the steering wheel repeatedly as the others roared at his expense.

Somewhere over the Atlantic

Maggie sat at the front of the private jet, her hands duct-taped to the armrests. Her face throbbed in agony and every breath proved painful, a fresh beating delivered after she had been thrown into the seat, her captors evidently angry after receiving a phone call. She had no doubt it was because of what had happened back at the building where they originally held her. It had to have been Dawson and the others. And from the amount of gunfire she had heard before she was taken away in the helicopter, she had a sense a lot of these bastards were now dead.

Which made the pain a little more tolerable.

What she didn't understand was why was she still alive. The display on the cabin wall in front of her showed their ETA to Moscow and their position on the map with their planned course. They were already over the Atlantic, though it didn't matter—any interception in the air was impossible. If the pilot didn't want to land, he wasn't going to land. The only option left to any Air Force pilot would be to blow them out of the sky, which they obviously weren't going to do.

All she could hope for now was that when they landed, the Russian authorities would rescue her. The country was as corrupt as hell, though there was some semblance of law and order there. And the American government could certainly put pressure on them, especially public pressure that might embarrass the Russians into acting. After all, this was the Russian mob. She was certain of that now. These weren't street-level gangsters. Most of the people she had seen wore suits, and the building she had been held in seemed to be completely controlled by them. Not to mention the fact they were flying around in helicopters and private jets.

No, this was definitely organized crime, and she recognized enough words to know that these people were Russian before it had been confirmed by their ultimate destination. Almost any other country, and she would be expecting Dawson and the others to rescue her. But Russia was an entirely different beast. Whatever it was her fiancé and his comrades had done this evening couldn't have been officially sanctioned unless the President himself ordered it, Posse Comitatus still in effect even if the family of American soldiers were involved.

Whatever had happened tonight, it was off the books, which she had a feeling was tacitly approved by her boss, Colonel Clancy. But Russia was another thing, and as much as she wanted to be rescued, it was too dangerous. She didn't want anyone else dying because of her, and she didn't want anyone's career sacrificed to save her. She should already be dead. If the others hadn't escaped thanks to Vanessa's quick thinking, she would have been shot hours ago, and she was willing to die if it meant the others lived.

The man in charge appeared in front of her, pulling on a pair of leather gloves, and she began to sob.

"Now we will discuss just who you are, and who those men were who tried to rescue you."

She closed her eyes and prayed to God for death as the first blow landed.

Fayetteville Police Department
Fayetteville, North Carolina

"Everybody quiet!" shouted somebody as the TV in the detectives' squad room was turned up, a breaking news report showing a massive police presence at an office tower in New York City. Detective Sneider sat at his desk, staring at the lined-up body bags as the reporter indicated that a rival gang had hit what was suspected to be a Russian mob stronghold.

Lance grunted. "New York City Russian mob hit the same night as our little happening? Coincidence?"

Sneider held up a finger, cutting her off as a security guard appeared with a microphone held in front of his face. "They forced me to let them on the roof, but when I heard what they were doing, I would have let them anyway. They were trying to save some woman who was kidnapped and being tortured. These were the good guys. The bad guys are in that building over there." The man pointed.

"And did they rescue the woman?"

The man shrugged. "I have no idea, but I hope so. We need more people like them. These Russian mob guys have been sitting there in that building all this time and the police do nothing, the courts do nothing. The government just sits by while people die on the streets. That's why people take action themselves. We need more guys like this killing scum like those Russian bastards. Maybe then it'd be safe to walk the streets at night."

The interview cut away, somebody back at the studio possibly fearing a lawsuit over what had just been said that was likely going to result in an official complaint from the Russian embassy about bigotry. But the guy was right. Too often, the police knew where the bad guys were, knew who they were, but because of the law, there was nothing they could do to touch them. They could only hope to catch them in the act, and then far too often, good charges were reduced to next to nothing in plea deals to save court resources, or some technicality resulted in the perp walking.

It was enough to drive someone mad. And he had seen too many of his friends resign, especially over the past few years. Elected officials, the press, the activists, were only too happy to always point the finger of blame at a police officer when a criminal was shot committing a crime. Police weren't the problem. Yes, some individual officers were. Every profession had its racists and bigots, and they should be weeded out and punished appropriately, but this out-of-control reaction that wasn't being challenged by politicians and media pundits, too terrified of being canceled, was ridiculous. It wasn't as if after what was discovered at Abu Ghraib, every politician in the land and every news organization demanded the entire American military be disbanded because of the actions of a few soldiers.

It was nonsense, and it was yet another thing that pissed him off about the military—the double standard. How many innocent people had died on their watch, yet nobody demanded they be sanctioned? Mistakes happened in policing, and often those mistakes were tragic. But just like on the football field, when you went to the instant replay and in slow motion saw that the referee had made a mistake, it wasn't reality. Real life didn't take place at 1/10th speed. Shooting incidents often unfolded in a matter of seconds. That meant instinct, and that meant the potential for mistakes. When the ref made a bad call, you didn't fire all the refs. The potential chaos on the field should be obvious to anyone. The same was true for policing. Just because a mistake was made didn't mean you fire the entire damned team.

He growled.

Lance regarded him. "Are you in your head again?"

He grunted. "Am I that obvious?"

She pointed at his can of Diet Pepsi crushed in his grip. "At least you finished this one."

He released it, his white knuckles rapidly returning to normal as he laughed. He pointed at the screen. "So, are you thinking what I'm thinking?"

She glanced over her shoulder. "What? That our Army buddies hopped on a plane and paid the Russian mob a visit?"

"Yup."

"Then yes, I guess I am thinking what you're thinking. What do you want to do about it?"

He shrugged. "Not my jurisdiction. I say we just focus on our little local problem, and then as soon as the FBI decides they're taking over, which I'm guessing they already have and nobody bothered to tell us, we can move on to one of our petty little local gang cases."

Lance turned in her chair and stared at the screen, more body bags being brought out. "If it is the guys from Bragg, I really hope they succeed."

Sneider was shocked to find himself agreeing. "So do I."

Somewhere over the Atlantic

Maxim stared down at the bloodied mess and frowned.

"Is she dead?" asked one of his minions.

If she were, it would be unfortunate. She had more information to give. Of that, he was certain. She had already revealed that her fiancé was in the American Army, obviously stationed at Fort Bragg, but beyond that, she had revealed little. His name was Burt White. She worked at some retail store on the base called The Exchange and knew little of what her future husband did, beyond that he was involved with logistics. Yet he sensed she was lying to him. She had held out longer than any woman he had ever interrogated, and when she finally did break, he was a little disappointed, though pleased she was finally talking.

But the information was utterly useless. And when he challenged her on little details about her job, about her fiancé's job, there were hesitations, as if she were searching for a believable response. If those who had hit their New York offices were associated with her Army fiancé, then there was no way in hell he was logistics. They were hit by pros who had somehow managed to not only track him, but determine exactly what room this woman had been held in, and then

169

killed dozens of his men without taking a single casualty of their own, if the latest reports were to be believed. They had to be Special Forces, and with it being Fort Bragg, it meant Delta.

He had spent the past fifteen minutes attempting to confirm what he feared, yet she had insisted he was logistics. All that she had given up was that Delta being at Fort Bragg was a secret that everyone knew, but she had no idea who any of them were. Again, useless information.

He pulled off one of his gloves then reached down with two fingers and pressed it against the side of her neck, confirming a pulse. "Well, she's alive."

"She won't be much longer if you keep beating her like that. If she knew anything, she would have told you. Even a man couldn't hold out that long."

Maxim grunted. "Perhaps, but I don't believe her. That team that hit us was no rival gang. I'm betting they were Delta."

"Shit, boss, if they were, we could be in for a world of hurt. What are we going to do?"

"We're going to do nothing. Once we're in Moscow, they can't touch us. It would be an act of war. We'll enjoy the hospitality of our Russian brothers, the warmth of our Russian sisters, and fill our bellies with real Russian food and vodka. Then, when this blows over in a few weeks, we'll head back to New York and rebuild."

"But what about those Special Forces guys?"

"We'll just make sure the authorities know who is behind it, and their commanding officer will put an end to it. If there's one thing the Americans don't want, it's the world knowing their own soldiers are playing vigilante."

The Unit

Fort Bragg, North Carolina

Mickey stood in front of Clancy's desk. His commanding officer yawned heavily, glancing again at the clock on his wall, and yet again shaking his head. Mickey respected Clancy. He was a soldier's soldier who understood the code they lived by, and Mickey had no doubt Clancy would understand exactly what was going on now. The man pressed the tip of his index finger against the stack of envelopes just handed to him.

"And these are?"

"Official letters of resignation along with the proper paperwork."

"For whom?"

"BD, Atlas, Niner, Spock, Red, and Jagger."

Mickey held up another half-dozen envelopes. "This is my letter of resignation and those of the rest of the team, should it prove necessary. Everything's backdated to yesterday." He lowered his voice. "BD wanted to talk to you personally, Colonel, but he didn't want to risk there being anything that could be tracked back between the two of you."

Clancy grunted, tossing a hand toward his laptop. "You do realize that you guys are the lead story on pretty much every newscast and every website worldwide?"

Mickey squinted slightly. "Isn't it our actions that are the lead story, not us?"

Clancy gave him a look. "Fortunately for you, this is being chalked up to a well-organized attack by a rival gang, but unfortunately for you, they've got a witness who says he spoke to you and that you told him you were there to rescue a kidnapped woman. If they figure out who that woman was, then they could track it back here."

"Maggie has been taken out of the country, sir. There's no way they'll be able to figure out it was her."

"And if the Russian mob decides to tell the media, just to get you guys in trouble?"

Mickey shrugged. "Then they'd be admitting to her kidnapping, the murder of Joanne, the attempted murder of the others, the murder of a doctor and police officer at the hospital, not to mention the attempted assault on the hospital. And besides, the only proof they could offer up would be Maggie herself. Nobody would believe them otherwise." He indicated the stack of envelopes. "And if things truly go south, you and the Unit are protected. We're private citizens acting on our own, and no US Army equipment was used."

"None?"

"Everything was supplied by a friend, with financing from special friends."

Clancy chewed his cheek, staring at him. "Special *academic* friends?"

Mickey smiled slightly. "You could say that, sir."

Clancy cursed. "Every damn time I think we're even with them, they go and do something like this and tip the scales back in their favor." He sighed and leaned back, folding his arms. "Just what's the plan now, Sergeant?"

Mickey hesitated. "Do you really want to know?"

Clancy held up both hands. "No, you're right, I don't want to know." He eyed the stack of envelopes. "I can already guess where they're headed if the sergeant major thought these were necessary." He drew a deep breath, staring at Mickey. "Do I want to know what the rest of you have planned?"

Mickey smiled. "Nothing to worry about, Colonel. We'll be standing vigil with Spock's family."

"Uh-huh, armed to the teeth, I suppose."

Mickey grinned. "Do you really want to know?"

Off-the-books Operations Center

Outside Bethesda, Maryland

Leroux frowned as he scanned the new information Tong had discovered.

"What is it?" asked Fang.

Leroux shook his head. "Bad news."

Fang dropped in a nearby chair, turning to have a clear view of all the security monitors. "What?"

"Sonya has figured out the connection. This Minister Novak, who had the flight declared diplomatic at the last minute, has a son who lives in New York City named Maxim."

Fang's eyes widened. "Wait. In those briefing notes Sonya put together, didn't it say the name of the guy they suspect is the leader of the Russian mob in New York City is some guy known as Maxim?"

Leroux confirmed it with a nod. "Yup. The man we're after, the man who has Maggie, is the son of a senior Russian minister."

Fang cursed in Chinese, sending Leroux's mind off on a tangent, wondering just what a Chinese curse was. "If their target is the son of the Minister of

Energy, then he's protected. We can't touch him without there being a significant response. There's no way the guys are coming out of this alive. We have to warn them. We have to stop them."

Leroux sighed, shaking his head. "I'm afraid it's too late for that."

Somewhere over Continental Europe

Atlas groaned for the umpteenth time. "When we get out of this, my fists are having a word with Dylan's face."

Niner, three inches from his nose, chuckled. "I sat in business class once. It's not as good as you think it is."

Atlas grunted. "Anything's better than this."

Niner shrugged in the dim light provided by a single bulb, powered by a battery designed to last not much longer than the length of the flight. And to preserve their sanity. What Atlas could describe only as a coffin in disguise was a method that Kane assured him the CIA regularly employed to smuggle people in and out of different countries. He had used his contacts to have the three containers, now occupied by six Bravo Team members, declared as diplomatic pouches. It meant that if the Russians wanted to obey international law, they couldn't touch them, they couldn't even scan them.

Apparently, these containers were sent back and forth across the Atlantic daily, so there was nothing out of the ordinary in this particular shipment, beyond the fact the containers were occupied and held two people each instead of the usual one. It made for cramped quarters for their ten-hour flight, and he had the unfortunate privilege of sharing the confined space with the chattiest person on the team.

When he had complained, Kane had pointed out the obvious. "Biggest guy goes with the smallest guy. It only makes sense."

Niner had hugged him hard. "This will give us a chance to *really* get to know each other."

The first groan of a long ordeal had erupted in response. "What I don't understand is why you two get to fly like regular passengers."

Kane put an arm around Sherrie. "Well, as much as I'd love to snuggle up with this cutie for ten hours, not only would my best friend disavow me, but I don't have to. We both have iron-clad covers."

"Really? After that mess in Moscow, you still think you're safe?"

Kane batted a hand at him. "For such a handsome man, you're so naïve."

Niner had patted Atlas on the chest. "He is handsome, isn't he?"

"Dreamy," agreed Spock.

"They never identified who we were," explained Kane. "And we have some people on the inside who managed to change our facial recognition mapping points in their database. Unless we happen to run into the same officers involved, we're golden."

The only concern Dawson had expressed was one they all shared. "And if you do happen to run into that one wrong person who recognizes you, what the hell happens to us?"

"The same thing that's going to happen regardless. Several vehicles from the embassy will meet the aircraft on the tarmac, the diplomatic cargo will be

J. ROBERT KENNEDY

offloaded, paperwork will be signed by embassy officials, and then you'll be taken to the embassy where one of our people will let you out."

Atlas frowned. "You're sure about that? They're expecting us? They're not going to say, 'Oh well, let's check in the morning,' because if I spend even a minute longer than I have to with Chatty Cathy, I'm going to be Hulk-smashing some things."

Everyone had laughed, and Kane had reassured him there was no chance of that happening, and now they were less than an hour away from landing, if everything was on schedule.

Atlas growled. "My back is killing me."

Niner reached over with one arm and began kneading Atlas' lower back.

"Just what the hell do you think you're doing?"

"Giving you a massage."

"Did I ask for a massage?"

"You didn't need to. I'm your best friend. Of course I'm going to help in your hour of need."

"I think that massage is going a little low, mister. That's not my back, that's my ass."

"And what an ass."

"Get back on your side of this coffin or I'm going to rip that arm off and beat you with it."

Niner gave Atlas' ass a pat then withdrew his arm. "You're so moody."

"You would be too if you were trapped for ten hours with you."

Niner shrugged. "I doubt it. For one thing, there'd be twice as much room, and secondly, the conversation would be sparkling."

"Huh. Well, one thing's true, there would be a whole lot more room in here."

178

Niner patted Atlas' massive pecs. "Maybe you should lay off the weights and drop half a ton of muscle."

Atlas stared at his friend. "What, become a puny little girly man like you?"

Niner grinned. "It does have its advantages."

"Such as?"

"Well, for one, I can fit through a doorway without having to turn to the side, and I can escape down narrow alleyways that would have you looking like the cork on a wine bottle."

Atlas frowned, staring down at his body. "You may have a point, but I've been lifting weights since I was a teenager. I have no intention of giving it up now just so that the next time I'm forced to spend ten hours in a coffin, I have more room to share with whoever I'm stuck in it with."

Niner shrugged. "Your choice. I know you define yourself by how much you can bench press, and while Vanessa and I both love your rippling muscles, we also love your witty repartee and hand-to-hand combat skills, though for different reasons."

Atlas' eyes narrowed. "Huh?"

"Well, I like how you kick ass, and she likes how you smack ass."

Atlas shook his head. "I'm going to tell her you said that."

"Go ahead. She's the one who said it to me."

Atlas' eyes shot wide. "Are you serious?"

Niner grinned. "Ask her. I dare you."

Their CIA-issued light flickered then failed. Atlas cursed, then cursed again when Niner snuggled up close to him.

"I'm scared. Hold me."

Atlas tossed his head back, banging it against the crate. "Kill me now."

Kane sipped his sparkling water as Sherrie snoozed beside him, her head on his shoulder. Their cover was once again boyfriend and girlfriend, which was a lot of fun. She was gorgeous, had a terrific personality, and he trusted her implicitly, as she did him. Not only were they friends, but she was his best friend's girlfriend, which always made these ops fun if they were on camera and Leroux was being forced to watch the lovey-dovey things they did together to maintain the cover.

Today, however, there would be no cameras monitored at the airport, at least not by his team. The goal today was to get in with nothing suspicious detected. He and Sherrie would clear customs and head to their hotel. Dawson and his team would be liberated at the embassy, provided with new identification papers prepared in-house, then they would rendezvous in Kane and Sherrie's suite where care packages should be delivered, along with, ideally, an update from Leroux on where their target might be.

All comms had been scrapped before they boarded, and they were incommunicado. World War III could be breaking out over what had happened in New York City for all he knew. He wasn't even willing to risk his secure messenger until they were away from prying eyes. His watch had gone off, indicating an urgent message on his private network, likely from Leroux, but he couldn't risk checking it, for he had no doubt the Russian FSB had at least one agent on the flight because of the diplomatic cargo. They would be watching for anything or anyone out of the ordinary that might suggest there was a reason to finally intercept the crates that continually flew back and forth. And netting two CIA operatives, including one as high profile as him, might be considered worth the international row it might cause.

So, he kept himself in the dark, sipping his Perrier, enjoying the lavender scent of Sherrie's hair, and closed his eyes, slowly drifting off as he pictured Fang, the woman of his dreams, the woman who had saved him from a destructive path. He recalled what he had done when he thought she was dead, and understood completely what motivated Dawson and the others. Never mess with someone's family. Never mess with their loved ones.

Especially if they were Special Forces.

You wouldn't live to regret it.

Embassy of the United States of America

Moscow, Russian Federation

Dawson was certain he had just finished the longest ten hours of his life. He stretched, attempting to work the kinks out, but he feared it would be some time before he would recover physically from the long ordeal. He shared the misery with Spock, and after some initial shop talk, they had both managed to fall asleep for most of the flight, leaving him alone with his nightmares until he finally woke in a sweat, still alone with his thoughts as his friend slept for another hour.

The nightmare scenarios over what could be happening to Maggie were unfortunately based upon personal experience. He had seen what was done to hostages, especially women. The imagery had him nearly in tears until he forced his mind to switch focus, and instead he fantasized as to what was about to unfold. He would find her, rescue her, kill everyone that got in his way, and then, when he finally got his hands on those who had harmed her, deliver brutal retribution.

The fantasies had turned his anguish into a rage, which was far more comforting. He regarded Red, his friend bending over and touching his toes. "How are you feeling?"

Red slowly stood straight, extending his clasped hands high above his head, and thrust his hips forward. "I think I might be getting too old for this shit."

Dawson agreed. "I don't think anybody's young enough for that mode of transport."

"Somebody get me the hell out of this thing before I kill him!" boomed Atlas.

As the lid was finally opened on their crate, Niner sprang out of the box with a grin, carrying himself as if he had climbed inside mere minutes ago.

Spock cocked an eyebrow as he did side stretches. "Just how the hell did you manage to survive that so chipper?"

Atlas' arm reached up from the box, the rest of his body still hidden. Niner grabbed it and leaned back, hauling the big man to a seated position.

"We gave each other massages."

Atlas growled. "No, *you* attempted to give *me* a massage." He stared at him. "You tried to massage my ass."

"That should be familiar territory," muttered Jagger.

Everyone in the room, including the two men who had freed them from their confines, snickered.

Atlas rolled his eyes. "I'd protest if it weren't true." He climbed from the crate, wincing as he grabbed his back. "I think I'm going to have to go on medical leave, BD. This body was never designed for that."

Dawson agreed. "I think we're all going to need a day at the spa when this is all done."

Niner flashed a shit-eating grin at Atlas. "Ooh, couples' massages. How romantic."

Atlas shook a fist at the man. "Don't make me use you like a rolling pin to work out these kinks."

Niner leaped over the crate into the shocked Atlas' arms, extending his legs and arms out, as good as any planker. "Do with me what you must."

Atlas dropped him and Niner smacked against the floor, though Dawson noted the experienced warrior had relaxed and slightly extended his hands in front of him to absorb the impact. It was all fun and games between the two men, best of friends, and despite outward appearances, no one was ever out to truly hurt the other.

Dawson turned to one of the men that had opened the crates. "I assume we're at the embassy?"

"Yes, sir." The man pointed at a table in the corner. "We used the covers you provided to create your new identity papers and cellphones, each loaded with varying amounts of history, plus itineraries for the tickets you flew in on, and your return tickets for two days from now on different flights. You're all staying at the Izmailovo Gamma. Men matching your descriptions"—he eyeballed Atlas—"which in some cases wasn't too easy to find, have already checked in to your rooms."

Niner elbowed Atlas in the ribs. "Good thing a passport is only a head shot, eh?"

Atlas shoved Niner, sending the little man flailing across the room, Jagger and Spock catching him. Niner straightened his shirt. "Man, spend ten hours with a guy in a confined space, you'd think he'd treat you a little better, especially after some of those air biscuits he floated."

Atlas shifted uncomfortably. "That's not my fault. I couldn't control it."

"I managed to. Did you hear a single unwanted eruption come out of my body?"

"If we're discounting that mouth of yours, then no, but in my defense, Vanessa was experimenting on me with new gumbo recipes. You know how my body sometimes reacts to spicy food."

Jagger rolled his eyes. "Yeah, yeah, your body's a temple. You're going to have to loosen up a bit, what with Vanessa being a chef. She's going to be insulted if you resist her food."

Atlas sighed as he inspected his new ID then patted his stomach. "Yeah, I might have to have my six-pack reduced to a four."

"Heaven forbid," muttered Red as he set up the Face ID on his phone. "Try being married to a woman who loves to bake. I gave up the whole six-pack idea years ago. The last time I could count all my abs, I was on the ISIS diet."

Dawson chuckled as he confirmed his own ID was as flawless as he expected. "That was the last time I saw you with hair too."

Atlas eyeballed Red's chrome dome. "Glad you shaved that thing back off. That fuzzy red tennis ball was creeping me out."

Red ran a hand over his shaved scalp. "Yeah, we Belme men have been cursed for generations. You should see photos of my grandfather when he was younger. The dude had a ginger fro. It was hilarious."

Atlas eyeballed Red for a moment. "I'll give you a full month's pay to see you with a fro."

Red pointed at Atlas' stomach. "Turn that six-pack into a keg, and I'll grow my hair out."

Atlas stared down at his beloved abs. "The price is just too high for some things, but when we get back from this mission, I'm breaking out Photoshop."

Niner grinned. "I think you'd look like Beaker from the Muppets."

Everyone laughed as they were led from the room to a more comfortable one just down the hall with chairs.

"You'll be let out individually as if you were people who came in from the street to conduct business here. The Russians shouldn't harass you on your way out. If they do, then your covers are most likely already blown. Also, we've got spotters. If you pick up a tail, you'll receive a text message on your phone saying, 'Are you up for cheeseburgers when you get back?' Reply, 'Absolutely,' if you want us to do nothing, or 'Sounds good,' if you want us to attempt extraction."

Niner held up a finger as he settled in a chair beside Atlas. "Attempt?"

The man shrugged. "You learn not to make promises in this business. Depending on how horny they are to hang on to you, we might not even be able to make the attempt. But from the briefing I received, nobody knows you're here, so they're likely not actively looking for you. Wear the ball caps and sunglasses, and you'll be fine. Do whatever you're here to do, keep your faces off-camera while doing it, and you should be able to use those tickets to leave. If not, call the embassy switchboard and ask to speak to Mr. Reynolds in Agricultural Affairs. He's in your contacts. As soon as the call is put through, each of your cellphones will be silently pinged so we can get locations on you. Hopefully, it won't come to that." He looked at the room. "So, who's first?"

Dawson was about to indicate he was when Atlas raised a hand. "I'll go. I stick out like a sore thumb in Russia, so I might just provide a distraction if they're watching for anything unusual."

Dawson chuckled. "Yeah, you don't exactly blend on the streets of Moscow." He shook Atlas' hand as the big man rose. "Just stick to your cover and you'll be fine. We'll see you at the hotel."

Atlas headed for the door with the other embassy staff member and jerked a thumb over his shoulder at Niner. "Make sure he's next. That way if they do arrest me, I can throw him under the bus and make an escape."

Niner looked him up and down. "You're not escaping anyone. I've seen you run. I think you just want to be alone with me in a prison cell."

Spock cocked an eyebrow. "You do realize there's no way you'd survive."

Niner batted a hand. "I'm not afraid of a Russian prison."

Atlas grinned. "I don't think that's what he was talking about, little man."

Embassy of the United States of America, Main Gate

Moscow, Russian Federation

Instinct dictated that when attempting to avoid cameras, one should keep one's head down, and while that might keep a camera from catching an image of a face, it also drew attention. As Atlas cleared the gates, he nodded at one of the Russian guards on the opposite side, and made it a point to keep his chin level. He spotted a taxi and raised his hand, executing a loud two-finger whistle. The cabbie cut across two lanes of traffic and, moments later, Atlas was safely inside, his sunglasses removed as they headed for the Izmailovo Gamma Hotel.

As they passed the embassy gates, he spotted Niner talking to one of the Russian guards, and a lump formed in his throat. He resisted the urge to look back, instead saying a silent prayer for his best friend, a man so different from him, he sometimes wondered how the hell they had become inseparable. Thank God Vanessa liked him, because somehow they had become a package deal. Now that Niner finally had a steady girlfriend, he found himself missing the little guy, though Angela and Vanessa had hit it off, so double dates and get-togethers at each other's houses were now frequent. The teasing was relentless, especially around the guys, but sometimes he'd find himself driving alone in his car thinking back on something Niner had said or done, and would piss himself laughing.

A police car sped past, its siren wailing, its lights flashing, and Atlas' chest tightened for a moment before he dismissed his concerns. If they had arrested Niner, it wouldn't be local police involved. He stared at his phone, doom scrolling the Twitter feed set up for his cover, the sausage party where everyone was talking, but no one was listening, depressing. He had once enjoyed social media, but had slowly soured to it. And once he had heard Professor Acton's theory on the binary society it was creating, he had pretty much divorced himself from it. He didn't want any part in dividing America further than it already was. He still had his accounts where he kept in touch with friends and family, but anything political, he blocked. He no longer gave that thumbs-up on anything he liked. The social networks were now a tool, and nothing but. He was done being their pawn, though at the moment he'd kill to send a message to Niner to see if he was okay, but so far, there was no message from anyone asking him about cheeseburgers, which should mean his friend was safe and well.

Niner pointed down the street. "So, just around the corner?" The guard nodded and Niner smiled, patting him on the arm. "Thanks, buddy. You just saved me a lot of hassle. I was going to go the other way," he said, jerking a thumb over his shoulder.

The guard gave a curt bow. "My pleasure, sir. Enjoy your stay in Moscow."

Niner grinned. "You can count on it. Beautiful city, friendly people." He headed in the direction the guard had indicated a taxi stand could be found. Niner's philosophy had always been that when you knew you were being watched, you should blend, and if you were playing a naive tourist in a foreign city, it meant asking for directions when it made sense to do so. And only a Westerner would think to ask a cop—in Russia they were avoided like the plague.

He had spotted Atlas passing by in a taxi, which had him relieved. It should mean his friend would make it safely to the hotel, and if the two of them, the two most distinct of the six here in Russia, could reach the destination unmolested, then it should be a cakewalk for the rest.

He rounded the corner, and as promised, there was a hotel with a taxi stand just up the street from it, a gaggle of drivers chitchatting. Niner raised his hand from across the street and one of them spotted him, waving back. The cabby hopped in his car, pulled a U-turn, and Niner climbed in. "Izmailovo Gamma Hotel, please."

"No problem," replied the cabby as he put the vehicle in gear and pulled away from the curb. The man glanced in his rearview mirror. "So, where are you from?" he asked in heavily accented English.

"United States."

The man squinted at him. "You're American?"

"Born and bred."

"You don't look American."

Niner laughed. "You obviously haven't been to America."

The man shrugged. "Maybe after I retire, I'll take my wife, but right now, no vacations for me. I have to drive the cab as many hours as I can."

"I hear you. The only time I ever get away is on business."

The man pursed his lips, staring in the mirror as they came to a stop at a light. "You definitely sound American, but you look, I don't know, Chinese."

"Korean, actually. That's where my family is originally from."

"Is it true half your country is Black?"

Niner shook his head, thinking of his buddy Atlas. "Nope, only about fourteen percent or so. There's actually more Hispanics than Blacks in America."

The man eyed him, puzzled. "What's Hispanic?"

Niner chuckled. "Let's just put it this way. Every country that encourages immigration has everyone you could imagine there, just living their lives, pursuing the American Dream."

The cabby pressed the accelerator as the light changed. "I don't think we have immigration in Russia. Everybody wants to leave here, not come here."

"Is it really that bad?"

"It depends on how you look at things, I suppose. You mentioned the American Dream. I don't know what that is, but I can tell you the Russian Dream I had when I was younger. We were finally a democracy, we had freedom, we had elections, we had capitalism, and a press that told us the truth. Things weren't perfect, but there was hope. Now that's gone. I get up in the morning, I kiss my wife, I eat a simple breakfast, and then I work for at least twelve hours. I get home, I kiss my wife, I have a simple dinner, then I relax in front of the TV with a vodka while my wife knits us clothes for the winter. Our apartment is old and drafty, and everything keeps getting more expensive. And by the time I'm eligible to retire, the government will have cut our pensions even more. My dreams are gone. I only pray that my children have the sense to get out of this godforsaken country before it's too late."

Niner felt for the man. Every time there was a mission involving the Russians, he thoroughly reviewed all the briefing notes, which brought him up to date on the latest goings-on in the country rapidly turning back into one of America's greatest enemies. It was becoming another prime example of how the public could be hoodwinked when the state controlled the media. The populations of countries like China, North Korea, Cuba, and Russia supported their government because they thought things were worse elsewhere, and that everyone was out to destroy what they had built, to steal their success for themselves.

Unfortunately, things weren't too much better back home now, though at least it wasn't the government controlling the message. It was two political dichotomies, so diametrically opposed to each other's point of view, that they would rather lie than concede the truth if it favored the other side. Sometimes it was discouraging when he thought about it. He and his friends put their lives on the line every day to protect their fellow countrymen, too many of whom wanted to tear down what had been built, who would spit on the institutions and the beliefs that had created the greatest country in the world.

He had to remind himself that those on the extreme, whether the left or right, were the minority. The un-silent majority, like here in Russia, woke up in the morning, kissed their spouse, ate a simple breakfast, and headed to work so they could pay the bills, support their family, and one day, if they were lucky, enjoy the fruits of their labor so they could grow old with their partner, and on that fateful day, kiss them goodbye at the end of a long life of hard work.

"Izmailovo Gamma Hotel as requested."

Niner smiled at the driver, handing a fistful of rubles through the divider, including an overly generous tip far more than the ride itself.

The driver's eyes bulged. "Can you Americans not do math?"

192

Niner laughed. "Take your wife out for a nice dinner. Show her a good time."

The man's eyes glistened and he reached a few fingers through the hole. "Thank you, sir. You are a kind and generous soul."

Niner squeezed the fingers. "You take care of yourself." He left the cab and headed into the hotel, his chest aching as he remembered his own childhood, and the long hours worked by his parents, how they had shielded him from their reality, keeping him ignorant as to how difficult their lives had been before they had finally established themselves. Then lost everything in the Great Recession, forcing them to start over.

The elevator door slid shut and he pressed the button for his floor, wiping away the tears that threatened to flow.

Man, I could use a hug. I wish Angela were here.

He smiled to himself.

I wonder what room the big guy's in.

Izmailovo Gamma Hotel Moscow

Moscow, Russian Federation

Kane and Sherrie sat on opposite sides of the king-sized bed, confirming everything they had requested was in the care packages dropped off only a few minutes ago by one of Kane's contacts. While Morrison had approved the use of their infiltration method, this op was still off the books. Russians were going to die, and while every attempt would be made to make sure only the guilty were among them, the Russian government would be pissed regardless, especially considering the intel that Leroux's team had gathered.

The man they were after was the son of a senior minister, and while kids could go rogue and be disavowed by their parents, it appeared to not be the case here. If you had written off your son for his criminal activities, you wouldn't arrange a diplomatic status flight to aid in his escape. No, this was a father who still actively supported his son, and perhaps was the true ringleader, manipulating things from afar as he set himself up for a luxurious retirement, funded by the ill-gotten gains of a criminal empire managed only superficially by his son. If the man proved to be the true puppet master, then he too would likely be among the dead, but for now, he was a conduit, not a target.

There was a knock at the door and Kane jerked his head toward it. Sherrie grabbed one of the Russian-made MP-443 Grach semi-automatic pistols from the bed, checking it was loaded, then peered through the peephole. She opened the door with a smile, saying nothing as Dawson stepped inside.

Kane glanced at his watch. "You're not supposed to be here for another ten minutes. You're lucky my trigger-happy friend didn't pump half a mag through the door."

Dawson chuckled. "Yeah, well, I was expecting you to answer, and the way you shoot, I'd have been perfectly safe."

Kane flipped him the bird, making fun of a fellow or former Delta operator's aim a running gag—there were no bad shots in the Unit, there were only varying levels of marksman. Dawson sat in a comfortable chair on the opposite side of the room.

"Any word from our friend and his team?"

Kane nodded as they resumed cataloging the duffel bags. "Yep, and you're not going to like it."

Dawson's eyes narrowed. "What did they find out?"

"The man who arranged the flight is the Minister of Energy in the Russian government, a man by the name of Mikhail Novak, and he has a son named Maxim."

Dawson's eyes widened slightly. "Wait a minute, isn't that the same name as our primary target?"

"Yup."

Dawson cursed. "You're kidding me."

"And if Daddy's arranging diplomatic flights for his son to escape justice, then he's fully aware of what the hell he is doing, and supporting it," added Sherrie.

Dawson grunted. "Well, he just got on my shit list."

Kane tilted his head toward Sherrie. "I highly recommend you never get on that list."

"I'll keep that in mind."

Dawson scratched his chin as he leaned an elbow on the arm of the chair. "Okay, Minister Daddy arranged for his son's escape. For him to arrange diplomatic status for that flight so quickly, it means his son has a direct conduit to him. I take it Leroux hasn't been able to find our target."

Kane shook his head. "Not yet. Without CIA resources, we're relying on unsecured cameras, and we're trying to avoid any hacking that might tip off the Russians that we're here."

"Then I think our next course of action is clear."

"Oh?"

"We need to pay Daddy a visit."

Kane frowned. "I was afraid you were going to say that."

Sherrie paused her inventory. "You do realize that this has international incident written all over it."

Dawson regarded her. "And you do realize that Maggie's life is at stake."

Sherrie shrugged. "Hey, I've got no problem with international incident if it means saving Maggie, but I think we all need to be clear what we're talking about. We're not paying this man a visit. We're talking about kidnapping the Russian Minister of Energy, forcing him to call his son to arrange an exchange, then once the exchange is complete, resisting the urge to take out everyone at the meet."

Dawson leaned to the other side. "That about sums it up. I don't see any problem with that."

Sherrie gave him a look. "You don't? Even if we manage to grab the minister, even if we arrange the exchange, you don't plan on killing him, especially if he's involved?"

"No, that would create an international incident."

"Exactly. Which means a man with all the resources of the Russian government, including their intelligence apparatus, will be left alive to begin asking questions, and I'd be stunned if it took more than twenty-four hours to figure out who Maggie is, which will lead straight back to you and the team. That paints some pretty big targets on you guys."

"Assuming they can identify us. Maggie leads back to Bragg, not the Unit."

"They'll have surveillance set up on her apartment in no time, which means they'd identify you and anybody who visits you and your team. I assume they're in and out of there all the time."

Kane chewed his cheek for a moment. "She's got a point there, and it might actually be worse if they can't identify you, because if Daddy is pissed off, they could just paint a target on Delta in its entirety."

Dawson tensed. "So then, what are you saying?"

"I'm saying, we have to let the son live."

Dawson cursed. "I want that little bastard dead, and I mean real slow like. I don't know who beat Maggie, but he certainly gave the order. He has to pay."

"And he will," assured Kane. "But not today. We grab the father, have him call his son, arrange the exchange, treat the man with kid gloves, make the exchange, walk away clean. Then a few months from now, maybe the son slips on a Twinkie in a stairwell and breaks his neck, something that can't be traced back to you or Maggie."

Dawson waved a hand. "You're right. I can't put the Unit at risk because of my vendetta. We do this clean. Nobody dies."

"Nobody dies today," corrected Sherrie. "It's open season a few months from now."

Dawson smiled slightly. "Of that, you can be certain."

Mokhovaya Street

Moscow, Russian Federation

Finding Minister Novak had proven to be the easy part. He was giving a speech at the Kremlin, undoubtedly espousing the financial benefits to Russia of the Nord Stream 2 pipeline, while privately bragging how it gave them near-complete control politically over Germany during the winter months—oppose Russia, get your natural gas cut off and freeze. Kane and Sherrie had managed to set up surveillance, giving them a clear view of the VIPs exiting a private entrance where their chauffeured vehicles were awaiting them. Unfortunately, the plan was dynamic. They had no idea whether there would be a motorcade, how many guards would be with the man, nothing. They were flying blind. All they could assume was that the car was armored, which didn't really matter—they had no intention of killing anyone.

"That's him there." Niner pointed at the laptop screen showing the video feed. A distinguished gentleman stepped out into the late evening sun, low on the horizon, and held a hand up to shield his eyes from the glare as he hurried down the stairs and climbed into the back of a Mercedes S-Class. Two black

SUVs formed up in front of and behind the Mercedes as they left the Kremlin grounds, the tinted windows giving no indication as to how many were inside. They could be facing two drivers, they could be facing half a dozen in each vehicle. And these were innocents, just men doing their jobs, not deserving to be killed because of a personal vendetta.

It made the job that much harder.

Dawson indicated with his hand for them to get underway, and Niner put the vehicle in gear, blending with traffic. Dawson leaned over and checked the sideview mirror to see that the vehicle operated by Red was behind them as he reviewed the plan in his head before ordering its execution. This had been the most likely scenario, so they were equipped for it, but a lot of things had to go right for things to not go horribly wrong.

He activated his comms. "This is Zero-One, you know what to do. Execute Plan Alpha, over."

A string of acknowledgments came through, and Niner pressed on the accelerator, slowly overtaking the small motorcade. The Russians apparently weren't too concerned about security, as there was no police escort clearing the way. Dawson eyed the traffic ahead, noting the green light.

"Control, Zero-One, turn that light red."

"Copy that," came Leroux's voice over the earpiece, and a moment later the light went amber then red, bringing traffic to a halt.

Dawson ignored the lead escort beside him and instead watched his sideview mirror.

"There he goes," said Niner, watching his own mirror. A moment later Spock, appearing drunk and disheveled, rounded the rear of Red's vehicle and stumbled up between the cars, knocking on windows with his hand held out, begging for change. He tripped at the front of the trailing SUV and while staging his recovery, placed a charge on the rim of the front tire. Using the vehicle's hood, Spock pushed back to his feet and patted it as if it had actively participated in him regaining his footing.

He continued forward with his act and Dawson watched as a small charge was tucked under the driver's door handle of the Mercedes so it wouldn't be spotted by anyone in the trailing vehicle. Spock continued his unsteady progress forward, again begging for loose change in Russian, before placing his final charge on the front driver's side tire of the lead vehicle. He then passed in front of Dawson's SUV, making brief eye contact before crossing the street and losing himself in the crowd. Spock's part was done. He'd rendezvous with Kane and await further instructions depending on how things went.

"Control, make it green." The light changed and the traffic surged forward. As they gained speed, Dawson eyed the road ahead. "Keep the lights green."

"Copy that," replied Leroux.

They were at full speed now, the traffic taking advantage of the string of green lights. "Take out vehicle three."

Jagger, sitting in the back, flicked the cover of the detonator switch and pressed the button underneath. Dawson peered in his sideview mirror as a small flash erupted from the front wheel, shredding it, bringing the SUV to a rapid halt, run-flat tires or not. It quickly lost pace as the driver guided the disabled vehicle to the side of the road, hopefully assuming a tire failure as opposed to an attack. The other two cars had no doubt received a transmission, and whoever was in charge would make the call on what to do next. If it were Dawson, he would give the order to continue, though on high alert, and he'd be radioing in their status so additional units could be sent just in case it wasn't an innocent flat.

It meant they had little time.

The traffic continued to flow rapidly ahead, and once enough distance was put between them and the disabled vehicle, eliminating any possibility those inside could join the fight on foot, he gave the order. "Take out vehicle one."

"Taking out vehicle one," replied Jagger, and another small detonation shredded another tire, bringing the motorcade to a screeching halt.

Dawson threw open his door and stepped out, a taser gripped in each hand. Both driver-side doors of the lead vehicle opened and two men stepped out. Dawson hit each in the chest, sending them shaking to the ground as Atlas did the same on the other side. Dawson continued forward, this time with his sidearm in hand, and checked the rear and front seats. "Clear!" he announced in Russian to obfuscate who they were. Within seconds, he and Atlas had all four men zip-tied and neutralized.

"Blow the second vehicle," he murmured into his mouthpiece. A bright flash and loud bang blew away the entire locking mechanism on the Mercedes' driver's door. The door swung open as Dawson repositioned, and he pressed the muzzle of his weapon against the dazed driver's temple. Dawson leaned over and found the passenger seat empty, and the rear seat occupied solely by their target.

"Hello, Minister Novak. We're not here to hurt you. We're here about something your son, Maxim, did. Please leave the vehicle immediately, and you will not be harmed, nor will your people."

The man cursed, remaining remarkably calm during the entire situation. "What the hell has that bastard done now?"

Dawson noted the derision in the man's voice. "Please exit this side of the vehicle immediately and I'll explain everything. You'll note we have used non-lethal force so far, and it's our intention to continue to do so as long as you cooperate."

The man shuffled across the seats then opened the rear door, stepping out. Dawson and Atlas each grabbed an arm and hustled him into their SUV. Moments later, both vehicles headed away from the scene, splitting off in different directions, the first stage of the plan a success so far.

Now the question was whether this man would put his son's life in danger to save his own.

Off-the-books Operations Center

Outside Bethesda, Maryland

Leroux leaned back, running his fingers through his hair, relieved. They had watched the successful operation through drone footage, and everything had gone off without a hitch, though now the entire city would be on alert. If they were to succeed in the ultimate mission, things had to proceed quickly.

The two vehicles involved carrying the team had reached their exchange points nearby, everyone now in new vehicles with no association with the previous, all exchanges made in parking garages with dead zones or completely overridden camera feeds. From all outward appearances, Phase One was completed, and if things continued according to plan, they might have Maggie back in as little as an hour.

"The city's going into lockdown," said Tong as she analyzed various feeds. "The longer this takes, the more difficult it will be for them."

Leroux folded his arms, his fingers drumming as he played out the various scenarios they could be looking at. The idea was that after the phone call was made, the exchange would occur, and the team would be extracted successfully through the prearranged tickets, and Maggie on a new one.

If everything went according to plan.

There was a coded knock at the front hatch entrance and Leroux waved off the others as he checked the camera. It was Fang returning from one of her patrols. He let her in then closed the door behind her, locking it.

"We might have a problem," she said as she headed deeper into the container and joined the others.

Leroux tensed at her words. "What? Did our friends come back?"

She shook her head. "No. They don't have the balls for that, but I was thinking. The last report we had was that Maggie was badly beaten."

"Yes?"

"Well, our plan is to just pull them out on regular flights. How's it going to look when a badly beaten woman is brought through the airport and onto a plane? That's going to draw a lot of attention."

Leroux's jaw dropped. It had never occurred to him, and she was right. They did have a problem. There was no way they could put her on a civilian flight, not without drawing so much attention that anyone with her could be flagged for further inspection. "Okay, we need a solution, and we need one fast."

Tong turned in her chair to face them. "Should we let the team know?"

Leroux shook his head. "No, they've got enough to worry about, and this only becomes a problem if they succeed. Let's not have them thinking about the next problem before they've got the current one solved. We'll have them rescue Maggie, and by the time that's done, the four of us are going to have a solution for them. Let's spitball. I'm open to any ideas."

"How big is the problem?" asked Tommy.

Leroux regarded him. "What do you mean?"

"I mean, are we coming up with a solution for all of them or just Maggie?"

Fang sat. "I can't see BD leaving Maggie alone."

Leroux shook his head as he returned to his chair. "No, there's no way, but Tommy's right. We're not looking for a solution for nine, we're looking for a solution for two. Dylan and Sherrie will use their covers to get out the same way they came in. The rest of the team can use their prearranged tickets."

Tommy raised his hand as if still in high school. Leroux indicated for him to speak. "Can we rely on those tickets? I mean, won't the Russians have the airports locked down and be double-checking everyone?"

Leroux shook his head. "You're forgetting one thing. Those tickets are for tomorrow, and if the exchange happens in the next few hours, the Russians won't be looking for their missing minister, he'll have already been released."

"But he's going to want justice, isn't he? I mean, they're still going to try to find out who kidnapped him."

"Oh, absolutely, but think about it. An expertly executed mission successfully kidnaps the Russian Minister of Energy, then releases him after exchanging him for a hostage his own son has taken. Would you expect them to hang around the city for another day then leave on previously booked civilian airliners? Or would you expect such a well-oiled operation to have a far more discreet and rapid exfil process already in place?"

Fang, an experienced Special Forces operator with the Chinese People's Liberation Army before her exile, stabbed a finger at Leroux. "You're right! There's no way we would conduct an operation like that without a foolproof method of extraction. They're going to pull out all the stops to try to catch our guys today, and once the minister is back in their hands, they're going to assume that if they haven't caught his kidnappers within a couple of hours, they're never going to."

"And if our assumptions are wrong?" asked Tommy.

"Then we'll know before they head to the airport. We'll be able to tell the level of security long before they're due to check in. If things haven't eased off, then we abort and use the embassy extraction plan."

"You mean take them out the way they came in?"

"Exactly."

Tommy's eyes narrowed. "Why aren't we just doing that?"

Leroux blasted air from between his lips. "Because the Chief said it was a one-time thing and not to ask again."

"Then how can we use that as a backup plan?"

Leroux smiled slightly. "You have to know the Chief. If lives are at risk, he'll make sure we can use the embassy route."

Tommy frowned. "I hope you're right."

Tong agreed with Leroux. "No, he's right. You do have to know the Chief. But if he can't or won't, I have no doubt Dylan has something up his sleeve if things go wrong."

"The Chief might not be thrilled with using the embassy route for the Delta team, but would he use it for Maggie and BD?" asked Tommy.

Leroux nodded. "He probably would."

Fang leaned forward in her chair. "There's still the problem of Maggie."

"What do you mean?"

"We don't know what condition she's in. All we know is she was severely beaten and more could have happened to her since. She might not survive ten hours in a crate. We need to get her out in comfort." Fang's eyes narrowed. "Does the embassy have an infirmary?"

Leroux shrugged. "I'm not sure, but it probably does."

"Well, if we got her onto embassy grounds, she could recuperate there for days or weeks, if necessary."

Leroux's head slowly bobbed. "That's an idea, though good luck getting BD to leave her there."

Fang exhaled heavily. "He might not have a choice."

Leroux pulled out his phone. "Okay, I'm going to contact the Chief and get this ball rolling, just in case."

CIA Headquarters

Langley, Virginia

Morrison sank into his chair, the sumptuous leather sighing with the relief his aging body craved. He inhaled deeply through the nose then held it for a moment before slowly exhaling through his mouth. His mind continued to race with the implications of being caught with the micro-drones in his desk before he had a chance to return them, and as he thought about how ridiculous the situation was, he chuckled. Kane had been true to his word. The drones and the controller had been returned last night, the package sitting on his doorstep not three hours after the carnage in New York City. He had been wide awake, sitting in the dark, watching the news, when a message had arrived on his phone.

Check the front door.

As soon as he had received the message, he had opened the front door and found the package sitting on the center of the porch, leaving him to wonder how long it had been there and how the hell whoever had delivered it had avoided his security. He had learned not to ask too many questions when it involved Kane or his methods. Kane was effective, and sometimes obeyed the rules, at least the limited rules those in his profession were required to follow.

As he lay in bed, struggling to get to sleep, he had concluded that whoever had delivered the package to his doorstep had used a drone, and it had him reevaluating the security at his residence and that of every other senior government official. What had happened recently in Baghdad had proven that drones could be used by non-military entities to attack a fixed position. And the drones capable of such attacks could be ordered on Amazon. The only challenging part was the explosives. He would talk to the head of his security detail to see what could be done about monitoring for drones and intercepting them before they became a danger.

But that could wait. He had a long day ahead of him, and was already exhausted, having managed little sleep. At midnight, he would return the micro-drones, yet they were the furthest thing from his mind. He had two of his operatives in Moscow off the books, half a dozen Delta operators so far off the books, they were off the reservation, and an American citizen kidnapped and apparently tortured, being held by the Russian mob on foreign soil that could only be considered hostile in the current political climate.

He was into this up to his neck. He had provided the micro-drones and provided the Delta team the means to secretly infiltrate Russia. If this went south, he was toast.

His computer beeped with a secure email notification. He logged into his secure email and found a priority message that had him cursing. The Russian Minister of Energy had been kidnapped off the streets of Moscow by unknown parties. The White House Chief of Staff wanted a briefing prepared for the afternoon threat assessment on who could be behind it, and what the implications might be.

Morrison closed his eyes, pinching the bridge of his nose.

I could tell you who's behind it, but you're not going to like it.

His cellphone vibrated with a message. It was Leroux. A pit formed in his stomach with the realization the hole he had dug himself was about to become far deeper. If Delta had indeed kidnapped the Minister of Energy, they were now the most wanted people in Russia, and even if they succeeded in rescuing Maggie, they had no hope in hell of getting out, at least not without his help. He planted his elbows on the edge of his desk and rested his head in his palms as he kneaded his scalp.

I should have said no, right from the get-go.

He had broken the cardinal rule. Don't get too close to those you work with. He didn't think of Leroux and his team as assets or Kane and his cohort as tools. He thought of them all as family. Family looked out for family. It shouldn't be that way. Not in his business, but it was, and to be frank, he had no desire to change it. And even if he did, there was one thing he refused to do, and that was to leave people hung out to dry.

He dialed Leroux's number and it was answered immediately. "What do you need?"

Tverskaya Street

Moscow, Russian Federation

Dawson sat in the rear seat of the clean Ford Expedition. His hostage sat blindfolded across from him as Niner drove. They had no weapons. No comms. Nothing. Everything had been left behind in the two SUVs they had used for the kidnapping operation. Kane's people would have already sanitized the vehicles and removed all the equipment used. If all went well, the Russian authorities would find nothing of use to trace who had been involved.

It also meant they couldn't defend themselves if they were intercepted, but that was fine. If the Russians caught up to them, there would be no point. He had no intention of killing Russians unless it was absolutely necessary.

Correction.

He had no intention of killing *innocent* Russians.

The scum he was after were fair game, though the others were right—they would have to wait.

He regarded his prisoner, assessing his body language, and he continued to find him remarkably calm. His breathing through the hood they had made him wear appeared steady and slow. He was sitting with his back in the corner, his left arm resting on the door frame, pressed against the tinted glass, his other hand resting on his leg. It was possible the man indeed was as calm as he appeared, though his physique and bearing suggested he was possibly in the forces at some point, and perhaps had been trained in how to read body language and how to use it to hide one's own tells.

Now that they were alone, Dawson dropped any pretenses. "I assume you speak English?"

"Of course. You're American?"

There was no point in denying it. The minister would know the moment the exchange was complete regardless. "I am, however I'm not acting on behalf of my government. I'm a private citizen."

"Who has apparently pissed off, or has been pissed off by, my son."

"Yes. My fiancée and three of her friends witnessed your son and an associate of his murdering someone. Your son then murdered one of her friends while they tried to escape, and kidnapped my fiancée and tortured her for information. Then when we attempted to rescue her, your son escaped with her and flew to Moscow on a flight you personally had designated as a diplomatic flight."

The man drew a deep breath through the hood, the material sticking to his face before it blasted away with a heavy exhale. "Do you have any children, sir?"

"Not yet."

"I'm sorry to hear that. Usually, they are such a joy, but some are bad seeds that should be thrown to the wolves rather than allowed to grow up and torment society." Another sigh. "And yet, they are still our children, and when possible, we protect them with the perhaps naive hope they will someday change." The man shook his head. "You're right. I did arrange for the flight to be declared a diplomatic flight, though I promise you, I had no idea of the truth. He merely said that there were dangerous people after him, and that if I didn't help him get out of the country, he would be killed. I had assumed it was a rival gang. It never occurred to me it could be anything like you described." The man turned his body more toward Dawson. "How can I help?"

"We want you to call your son and arrange an exchange."

The man chuckled. "Exchange me for your fiancée?"

"Yes. Why is that funny?"

"I'm not exactly his favorite person. I may help him from time to time, but it's never without a lecture, and a stern one at that."

Dawson frowned. "Well, that may be true, but I'm certain you can persuade him that if I kill you, any chance of you helping him in the future dies with you."

The man grunted. "I suppose you're right, and that's likely the only way he'll be convinced to do the exchange. Certainly his love for his father won't."

"Can you contact him?"

"Yes. I'll need a phone."

Dawson picked up a burner off the seat between them. "No games, or I'll do to you what your son did to my fiancée."

"No games. I want this to be over with as much as you do, but I promise you this. After you have your fiancée back, I'm disowning my son once and for all. Let the wolves have at him."

Unknown Location

Moscow, Russian Federation

Maggie sat in a vehicle. What type it was, she wasn't sure as she was gagged with her head covered by a hood. The high step inside, however, suggested it was an SUV or something similar. Certainly not a sedan. She was flanked on either side by men ignorant of the adage less is more when it came to cologne, odors assaulting her nostrils as she was forced to breathe through her nose.

In front of her, the driver was talking with the man in charge in the passenger seat. A word was said by the boss, then repeated questioningly by the driver. The boss growled, switching to English.

"This is why I only like to work with Russian-born people."

"I'm sorry, boss. You've met my mother. She insisted no Russian be spoken in the house. My father tried his best when we were alone, but you know how dedicated he was to his work."

The boss sighed. "And that's the only reason you have a job. He died saving my life, and I promised I would take care of you and your mother. But you have to learn Russian."

"I promise you, boss, I'll keep trying. But that word, what does it mean?"

The boss chuckled. "There's no real translation. You have to have lived with the language. It basically means 'false father.' He doesn't really care about me, he only cares about himself and any embarrassment I might cause him. He may have helped us today, but he doesn't realize I have other contacts I could have called as well. I could have accomplished the same thing without him. He has no idea how powerful I've become, how well connected."

"Yet you agreed to the exchange."

"I just want to be there to see his face when I tell that American to go to hell, and put a bullet in his fiancée's head."

Maggie whimpered, an elbow to her broken ribs the response. The voice changed as the boss obviously turned to face her.

"Yes, that's right, Maggie Harris. Your fiancé is going to see you die before I kill him and his friends."

Maggie's chest ached and she screamed into her gag.

Off-the-books Operations Center
Outside Bethesda, Maryland

Leroux sat in his chair, squinting at the different camera feeds from the drones they had deployed covering the hostage exchange. And their coverage was shit. The location had been dictated by Minister Novak's son. The moment they had the address, Kane had deployed multiple drones to the area, only to confirm what they discovered en route—it was an underground parking garage with no detectable camera feeds they could tap, and based upon the dilapidated state of the surrounding buildings, he had a sense this was not a good part of town. His gut told him that many a nefarious deal occurred at this location because of its dubious nature.

"Keep your eyes open for anything. Watch the shadows. The first sign this is a trap, I want to be able to pull our guys out."

Tong glanced at him over her shoulder. "You really think they'll pull out?"

"Not for a second, but at least they'll know what they're getting themselves into."

Tong pointed at the screen as a black SUV approached the entrance to the parking structure. The driver's window rolled down and Leroux snapped his fingers. "Make sure we get his face." Tong zoomed in, capturing a good shot of the man as he leaned out to press the button and get a ticket. "Tommy, run that and see if we can get anything on him."

"Got it." Tommy went to work as Leroux watched the vehicle disappear inside the garage.

Fang pointed. "Did you see that?"

"What?"

"Just as they pulled in, the driver waved at somebody."

"Rewind it."

Tong complied, and sure enough, the driver's left hand, resting on the open window frame, rose just as it disappeared out of sight.

"Has anything showed up on infrared yet?"

Tommy shook his head. "No, I haven't seen anything. You?" he asked, twisting in his chair and facing Fang, who was assisting.

"No, but if I was setting up this ambush, I would be keeping out of sight, and we only have a limited view of the first level. Everything else is underground."

Leroux chewed his cheek for a moment. "Do we risk sending in a drone?"

Fang folded her arms and pursed her lips as she thought. "I wouldn't."

"Why not?" asked Tommy.

"If the exchange is going to go smoothly, then sending the drone in is pointless and would only put that at risk. If the intention is to ambush our people, that's going to happen regardless."

"But we would know, and we could warn our people off."

218

Leroux sighed. "There's no way BD is not going in. He's in an up-armored vehicle, so if things go south, as long as he can make it back into the car, he should be able to get out, or at least hunker down until help arrives."

"This is awfully sketchy," said Tong. "If this were a regular op, we would never let it proceed."

"I agree, which is why we don't allow operatives on the ground to have a romantic interest in those they're trying to rescue. The agreement was two people each, so Dawson will go in with one of his men. That leaves six, including Dylan and Sherrie, to rescue their asses if needed."

Fang's head slowly shook. "For all we know, they've got fifty men in there."

Tommy threw up his hands. "Which is why we should send in the drone. We'd at least get a sense of what they're walking into."

"And we could end up killing Maggie in the process. We need to even up the odds a bit. Our people are the best. Highly trained and extremely well-equipped. We need to get them inside, undetected."

"Just how do you propose we do that?" asked Leroux.

Fang shrugged. "That all depends on you."

Chertanovo District, Exchange Point

Moscow, Russian Federation

Spock had insisted on driving Dawson to the meet. While anyone else was a better choice, purely for the emotional state they were both in, he wasn't about to deny Spock what might be their last opportunity for revenge should things go south. Right now, they had no way of knowing if Maggie was alive. Proof of life had been demanded, and denied. Unfortunately, he wasn't in control here, and he wasn't convinced the leverage they had by holding Maxim's father was worth anything if the relationship were as bad as described by the minister. Yet the meeting had been agreed to. They had to hope it was for the mutual exchange of prisoners, but expect the worst.

He just hoped Fang's plan worked.

"Here we go," muttered Spock as they turned, the parking garage ahead.

Dawson activated his comms. "This is Zero-One. We're about to enter the parking garage. Is everyone in position, over?"

The string of affirmatives came in over his earpiece.

"Control, Zero-One. Are you ready, over?"

Leroux replied. "We're ready to attempt this, but we've had no opportunity to test it. This could be an epic fail."

Dawson exchanged a look with Spock who shrugged. "No guts, no glory."

Dawson grunted. "Copy that, Control. Just do your best. Zero-One, out."

Spock rolled down the window as the car tipped forward and they descended the ramp. He pressed the button and a ticket spat out of the machine, the gate rising. He continued forward. Someone stepped out of the shadows, a PP-2000 submachine gun gripped in his hand, confirming what Control suspected—there had been somebody in the shadows.

The man appeared calm. He leaned in, peering into the rear at the prisoner, then stepped back and pointed. "Level three."

Spock acknowledged the instruction and pressed gently on the gas as Dawson lowered his window. The ambush wouldn't happen yet—the Russians would wait until they were in the bowels of the building. If things were going to go south, it would be for revenge, and revenge was always unsatisfying without a message delivered. They were going to meet their target, of that he had little doubt. The question was whether Maggie would be with them, and more importantly, whether she was alive.

"Put on your high beams."

Spock pushed the stalk forward, revealing a swath of the garage ahead of them. The garage was dimly lit, as most older garages were, the columns and half-height walls providing far too many places for hostiles to conceal themselves. Two infrared cameras mounted to the roof rack broadcast their signal to the others. Dawson had opted to not have the feed available to them in the car. If things went bad, he didn't want the Russians to know they were being watched, though he wanted the others to have every advantage available to them.

"One on our nine o'clock, behind the pillar," said Spock, his lips barely moving.

Dawson acknowledged the report. "One o'clock behind the half wall. Zero-Two, Zero-One. Are you guys picking up anything on infrared, over?"

"At least seven so far. I get the distinct sense they don't intend to let you leave. Recommend you abort."

Dawson grunted. "If we abort, they're definitely not letting us leave. We're committed now. Just follow the plan."

"Copy that."

"Level three," reported Spock, turning off the high beams and rolling his window up as they exited the winding ramp. A set of headlights shone at the far end and Spock slowed to a stop about 50 feet short, the two front doors of the SUV facing them opening simultaneously.

"Open your door but stay behind it," said Dawson as he pressed the button to roll his window up. He opened his door then stepped out. The passenger walked toward them several paces then stopped.

"Mr. White, I presume?"

Dawson suppressed the smile. Maggie might have talked, and he could never blame her for that, but she had still held out, and he couldn't have been more proud of her. "Yes. And you are Maxim Novak."

The man bowed his head slightly. "I am. I believe you have my father."

"He's in the back."

"Let me see him."

"Maggie first."

Maxim's fists clenched in the headlights, then relaxed. "Mr. White, you are in no position to make demands. Show me my father or I kill your fiancée." The man stepped back toward his vehicle, drawing a weapon from a shoulder holster. He opened the rear door and pointed the gun inside. "What's it going to be, Mr. White? Are you going to show me my father, or am I killing the woman you love?"

Dawson sucked in a breath, deep and slow, then jerked his head at Spock. "Get him out."

Spock stepped back, keeping his open reinforced door between him and the enemy. He opened the rear door, helped the minister out, then removed the hood from the man's head, tossing it into the back seat.

"Father, are you all right?" asked Maxim in Russian.

"I'm fine," came the curt reply.

"Did they hurt you?"

The man shook his head. "They didn't lay a finger on me. Give them the woman and let them go so I can report back to my people. Half the city is probably locked down right now."

Dawson tensed as Maxim inhaled quickly, his shoulders drawn back before he spat his reply. "You're in no position to tell me what to do, old man! I say what goes on here. I'm in control. I have the power. You're nothing! You're just a government stooge controlled by that puppet master in the Kremlin. You're pathetic!"

The minister held his tongue for a moment and thankfully remained calm, not taking the bait. "You're right, of course, son. This is your show. What would you like us to do?"

Maxim continued to glare at his father, his chest heaving, showing no signs of calming down. He had been triggered.

"This is Zero-One. Execute," whispered Dawson.

Off-the-books Operations Center

Outside Bethesda, Maryland

"This is Control. Executing," said Leroux as he indicated with a finger for Tommy to initiate the backup plan. Tommy tapped a key and leaned back, holding his hands up in the air in anticipation.

Tong stared at him. "Well?"

Tommy shook his head. "Nothing's happening."

Leroux cursed. "This is Control. Power grid takedown failed. I repeat, takedown failed."

Tommy leaned forward, furiously typing. "It looks like the Russians detected our hack and kicked us out."

Fang muttered something in Chinese. "Can you get back in?"

"I'm working on it! I'm working on it!"

"We need some sort of diversion if our people are going to get in there. If BD ordered the plan to be executed, it means that the shit has either hit the fan or it's about to."

Leroux pulled at his hair, all of his options playing out, each dismissed, his conclusion reached depressingly quickly as there were, in fact, too few. He turned to Tong. "Send in the drones."

Her eyebrows shot up. "Really? Won't that cause the shit to hit the fan?"

"He wants the shit to hit the fan, or it already has. If we send in the drones, it could distract them long enough for our guys to make entry."

"Okay, throwing shit at the fan." Tong sent in the drones and Leroux reactivated his comms as Fang took a seat to help control two of their four devices.

"This is Control. We're sending in the drones as a distraction. We're still working on the power."

"Copy that," replied Red, and he waited for a reply from Dawson or Spock. But none came.

Chertanovo District, Exchange Point

Moscow, Russian Federation

Niner and Atlas surged down the ramp to the parking structure, each hugging an opposing wall as one of the drones flew past and entered the dim interior. Somebody shouted in surprise and was joined by two others, gunfire erupting as they continued down the ramp. Tong's voice came in over their comms.

"One on the immediate left of the door, a second is ten meters at your eleven o'clock behind the pillar slightly to the left, a third is five meters in on the right, behind a half-wall. All are standing."

Atlas, on the right, took the lead as Niner slowed up slightly, the first target needing to be taken out not in his arc. Atlas reached the entrance, his suppressed Grach aimed at a sharp angle to his left. He squeezed the trigger twice then swung quickly to the right as he continued forward. Niner advanced, finding his target by the pillar still distracted by the drone that someone was expertly controlling. He double-tapped him as Atlas did the same to his target before they both pressed deeper inside.

Finding cover, Niner activated his comms. "This is One-One. Main ramp is secure, over."

The distinct thuds of gunfire above them had Maxim staring at the concrete overhead then aiming his weapon at Dawson. "You betrayed me."

Dawson shook his head. "I have no idea what's going on. Maybe it's the police."

"Bullshit!" Maxim's weapon swung toward his father, belching lead as Spock shoved the minister into the back seat, the open driver door absorbing the impact of the bullets. Maxim roared in rage as Dawson drew his weapon and advanced. "You just killed your fiancée!" Maxim redirected his aim at the back seat and squeezed the trigger twice.

"No!" cried Dawson as he sprinted forward, firing his weapon. Maxim dove into the back seat as the driver jumped behind the wheel. He hammered on the gas, the SUV squealing backward as more gunfire thundered above them, the team meeting stiff resistance.

"BD, we gotta go!"

But he didn't hear his friend. All he heard was the thunder, the thunder of the gunfire, the thunder of his pulse in his ears, the breaking of his heart with the realization that Maggie was dead and he had killed her. He emptied his mag in the retreating vehicle, his body on autopilot, but it was of no use. It was reinforced just like their own, and while the bullet-resistant windshield splintered, indicating his aim had been true, nothing got through.

The vehicle backed up the exit ramp, the screeching of metal as it scraped concrete fading as the distance grew.

"We have to get out of here, BD! Get in the damn car now!"

Still echoes.

"Sergeant Major!"

Dawson's head snapped toward Spock.

"Get in the car!"

Dawson climbed in and Spock hammered on the gas, following the them up the exit ramp.

"This is Zero-Five," said Spock. "No joy on the exchange. Our primary target might have executed Maggie. We're in pursuit now." He cursed as three men with sub-machine guns stepped in front of them, spraying bullets. Dawson, back in the game, his weapon already reloaded, reached out through the opening passenger's side window and fired as Spock pressed on the gas. Two of the hostiles stepped aside, their weapons continuing to spew lead as the bumper took out the third man. Dawson got a bead on one of the remaining gunmen and fired, taking him down. Spock cranked the wheel as they continued up the ramp, the third gunman emptying his mag into their rear end.

Niner's voice came in over the comms. "Suspect vehicle is approaching our position. Do we engage?"

"Affirmative. Take them out," replied Dawson.

Spock cursed and activated his own comms. "Negative! Do not engage! We have not yet confirmed Maggie is dead."

"What are we doing here?" demanded Niner. "Engaging or not?"

Spock turned to Dawson. "He fired two shots. We don't know if he killed her or not. But if we engage, she's absolutely dead."

Dawson was already certain she was, but if there were even the remotest possibility, he could never live with himself if he took that away. He nodded.

"This is Zero-One. Let them go. Everyone fall back to the rendezvous position. Control, make sure you don't lose them, over."

Leroux replied. "We're repositioning the drones now for pursuit. It looks like you've got locals coming into the area. Recommend rapid egress, over."

Spock hit the brakes as they approached the exit. Niner and Atlas both climbed in then he slammed on the gas again, sending them surging up the ramp and onto the city street.

Niner leaned forward between the seats. "We need to get out of this tin can fast. It's got more pock marks in it than a bad case of teenage acne."

Atlas jammed a finger between everybody, pointing ahead at some flashing lights. "Locals."

Spock cranked the wheel to the right, sending them careening down a side street. Dawson pointed ahead at a delivery vehicle. "Park in front of that. Dump all equipment except comms."

Dawson and the others stepped out of the heavily damaged vehicle and stripped out of their equipment, tossing it back inside.

Niner jerked a thumb at their hostage, who had had the presence of mind to put his hood back on when shoved in the back by Spock. "What about him?"

"We're done with him." Dawson leaned in. "Sir, we're walking away now. Please count to one hundred before removing the hood."

"I understand. And I'm sorry for what my son did. I pray your fiancée is still alive."

"Thank you, sir, but I'm afraid I will be forced to kill your son for what he's done."

"I understand. I would do the same if I were in your position."

All four doors slammed shut and they strode quickly toward the next street as sirens wailed behind them. This was no longer a rescue mission. Maggie was dead, of that he had no doubt. The rage he had witnessed in Maxim's eyes was the rage of a man acting irrationally. She was dead, despite Spock's offer of faint hope.

Now the vendetta would begin.

Chertanovo District, Rendezvous Point

Moscow, Russian Federation

Sherrie's fingers drummed on the steering wheel as she waited at the rendezvous point several blocks away from the scene. According to Leroux, locals were swarming the parking garage. The team had made it out successfully, but two of their drones had paid the price, though had delivered the distraction.

While the team getting out alive and unscathed was a success considering how many they had been up against, the mission was a complete failure. They hadn't retrieved Maggie, and the assumption was that she was likely dead. She understood Spock's faint hope that perhaps she hadn't been shot at all, but she didn't buy it. She had been listening, and everything had happened too fast. There was no way Maxim had the presence of mind to shoot into the rear seat and intentionally miss her when he discovered the betrayal. She was dead unless he was a horrible shot, but at that range you'd have to be blind to miss.

Her heart ached at the sorrow Dawson must be suffering. According to Kane, they had been through a lot over the past few years, and had finally begun moving forward with their lives again, their wedding plans back on.

And now this.

The question was, what should they do now? She couldn't see Dawson agreeing to let them leave the country without confirming Maggie was indeed dead, and she wouldn't blame him. If the roles were reversed, there was no way she would leave if it were her boyfriend. If they were to remain and seek that proof of death, there were only two ways she could think of to accomplish that. One was to use Maxim's father to convince his son to dump the body somewhere they could find it, likely with the understanding they wouldn't be pursued by Dawson and his men or the authorities, and the other option was to continue the pursuit and kill everyone involved until they found Maggie.

She had a feeling Dawson would opt for the latter, and his team would agree. All they had killed so far were foot soldiers. The revenge was unsatisfactory. The man in charge, Maxim Novak, had to pay the ultimate price for the death of Joanne and Maggie, and the wounding of Vanessa, and the terror she and Shirley would live with for the rest of their lives. Only his death would bring the closure Bravo Team and the extended family needed to move forward.

Kane emerged from around the corner carrying a box. He strode nonchalantly toward the SUV and indicated with a jerk of his chin for her to pop the rear hatch. She leaned forward and pressed the button, the hatch opening, and he placed the box inside before closing it back up. He climbed into the passenger seat, glancing in the back. "Nobody's arrived yet?"

"Not unless they can cloak themselves like the Jem'Hadar."

Kane eyeballed her. "Chris has turned you into a total geek, hasn't he?"

She grinned. "And don't you forget it." She eyed him. "Odd that you got the reference, though. Geek." She tilted her head toward the back. "What's in the box?"

"The two drones we lost."

Her eyes widened. "You went back for them?"

"Yeah. A rival gang wouldn't use drones. We want the locals thinking that what happened is domestic."

"Won't the minister set them straight?"

"He might, but after what just went down, he may think twice, and I don't want to give anyone a reason to question whatever story he might concoct. Remember, if he tells the truth, he has to admit his son is a Russian mobster who kidnapped and tortured an American citizen and brought her to Russia, which could make his position difficult. My guess is he'll claim he was kidnapped, doesn't know by whom, and will claim there was a shootout he didn't see because he had a hood on, and then he was set free by his captors, none of whom he ever saw. We left enough bodies in that garage that it'll fit the story, and the Russian authorities will chalk it up to a kidnap for ransom plot gone bad."

"Let's hope you're right. That would certainly make things easier for us all getting out of this shit hole of a country."

Kane's chin jutted forward. "There's Red and Spock."

The two men were walking at a brisk pace, their hands and arms moving animatedly as if they were having an argument. As they reached the SUV, they split to either side, both climbing in the second row, the doors slamming shut, the tinted windows concealing them from prying eyes outside.

Kane twisted in his seat to face them. "Everything good?"

"No problems," replied Red. "But that place is crawling with LEOs. If we don't get out of here soon, they're going to be spreading their net. Right now, they're still reacting."

Sherrie peered in the rearview mirror. "Here comes BD and Atlas." The two men climbed in the back.

"Everything good?" asked Dawson.

"We're just waiting on Niner and Jagger."

Atlas extended a finger forward. "Here they come."

Sherrie chuckled at the sight of Niner and Jagger stumbling toward them, putting on a great show of being floor licking pissed. Niner pulled open the door then climbed into the rear row as Jagger was pulled into the middle, the door slamming shut behind them.

"Let's get the hell out of here," said Kane.

"You don't have to tell me twice." Sherrie put the vehicle in gear and gently pulled away from the curb, making certain she did nothing to attract the attention of any of the police within their line of sight the moment she turned back on the main road.

Dawson activated his comms. "Control, Zero-One. Give us an update, over."

Leroux's voice filled their earpieces. "We have two drones tracking their vehicle. It looks like they're heading out of the city."

"Understood. Contact me when you have a final destination. Zero-One, out."

Sherrie continued to guide them away from the scene of the crime. She glanced in the rearview mirror. "Where are we heading?"

Dawson bit down on his cheek for a moment. "Wherever he's going, I have no doubt he's going to be there soon. I intend to find him and kill him, and I don't expect any of you to join me. This is personal."

"Damn right it's personal," said Spock. "I'm coming with you."

"So am I," rumbled Atlas. "He nearly killed Vanessa."

Niner jerked a thumb at the big man. "You know I go where he goes."

Red shrugged. "Shirley's going to have nightmares if I don't come home telling her she doesn't have to worry about him anymore."

Jagger's big lips were duck-faced in front of him. "Well, obviously I'm coming. I'll never hear the end of it if I was the only one who chickened out."

Dawson smiled at his men as Sherrie swallowed the lump that had formed in her throat. She stared back at the team with glistening eyes. "Well, I'm obviously going. I have to prove to my boyfriend how badass I am."

Kane sighed heavily. "Well, if she's going, I have to go because if something were to happen to her, I'd never hear the end of it from her boyfriend."

Dawson reached forward, grabbing them both by a shoulder and giving them a shake. "Excellent. Then how about you get us to some place we can hole up while CIA boy here gets us another load of equipment."

Kane rolled his eyes as he pulled out his phone. "Good thing the professors are bankrolling this, because this shit is expensive as hell, and each time I place an order for the same bunch of stuff, the price doubles."

"Doubles?" asked Niner. "Why the hell would it double each time?"

"Because there's a limited supply and their risk grows each time."

Niner cursed. "I'm in the wrong business."

Atlas grunted. "I've been telling you that for years. This is a man's business, not a mini-man's."

Niner glared at his friend. "You saw Ant-Man. He kicked ass."

"Ant-Man? Wasn't that the only Marvel movie you could have auditioned for without special effects?"

Niner flipped two birds at Atlas, the rest of the team roaring with laughter, the birds then shared with the group.

Kane held up a finger, silencing them all. "Yeah, it's me. I'm going to need another delivery ... I can't confirm that, but if it were us, what can you tell me? ... I see. Very well, how long? ... Okay, we'll see you in an hour." He ended the call and turned back to face the others. "My supplier, who's plugged into pretty much every organization in Russia, sounds nervous."

"Why?" asked Dawson."

"Because what just went down is heating up the air waves. You'll be happy to know the minister has been picked up and word went out that it's gang-related."

Sherrie breathed a sigh of relief as smiles spread through the vehicle. They might just get out of this alive.

Leroux's voice came through her earpiece. "This is Control. We have a final destination, and you're not going to like it."

Outside Moscow, Russian Federation

Leroux had been right. Dawson didn't like it. It turned out the final destination was a walled estate on the outskirts of the city. They had split into three teams again, and the riskiest part of the operation was about to begin. The two drones that had followed Maxim to the estate had been providing constant coverage of the grounds since then, and from all outward appearances, it suggested security was minimal, though Dawson had little doubt Maxim had called for reinforcements.

The question was, what did he have available to him here? This wasn't his base of operations. He certainly would have connections here, but would there be an obligation to send troops to protect him against a force that had just taken out at least a dozen on Russian territory, and even more on American soil? It was a question he didn't want to wait to see answered, which was why they were pressing ahead without wasting any time.

Leroux had managed to get them satellite photos of the estate, but little else. Routine scouting had revealed the entire perimeter was covered by video surveillance and motion detectors. Entry over the walls would definitely be detected, and Leroux's team had found no way to penetrate the security system from the outside. It was a closed system with no external digital access points, at least none they could detect. The only way to gain access was waiting at least another hour for a special delivery from Kane's people with the equipment necessary to bypass the perimeter sensors. It left the main entrance, where a wrought iron gate was manned by two guards sporting submachine guns.

"They're approaching the gate now," reported Niner through the comms. Niner and Atlas, both equipped with sniper rifles, were positioned on a hill opposite the estate, giving them a full view of the front lawn. They would provide cover against any surprises outside.

Dawson waved a finger toward the windshield and Red put the vehicle in gear, heading toward the estate. Everything had been planned out as carefully as possible, despite the lack of intel and the short timeframe. But there was one part that was absolutely critical that couldn't fail. He activated his comms. "Control, Zero-One. Are you ready?"

"Affirmative, Zero-One," replied Leroux.

"And it's going to work this time?"

"I'm assured it will."

"From your lips to God's ears."

"They've reached the gate," reported Niner.

The news caused Dawson to grip his weapon tighter. This was it. This was the end. He would either die here tonight, or leave having killed everyone responsible for what had happened.

And Maggie would be avenged.

Kane pulled up in a jet-black luxury British sedan, the notoriously unreliable brand having left him uneasy the entire drive here. The last thing they needed was an engine failure. He rolled to a stop in front of the gate that remained closed. He lowered his window as a guard emerged from the post, his submachine gun gripped tightly in his hands, his partner stepping in front of the car, his own weapon aimed directly at Kane.

"This is a private residence, turn around."

It was evident the man was on edge, either a participant in the events of earlier, or made aware of them. Either way, Kane kept both hands on the steering wheel. "I have a special order for Mr. Novak."

The man eyed him. "Special order? What the hell are you talking about?"

Kane jerked his head toward the rear seat. The man bent down and peered inside, his eyes bulging at the scantily-clad Sherrie sitting in the back seat. She waved coquettishly at him. The guard cleared his throat, stepping back, clearly aroused.

"I wasn't told she was coming."

Kane shrugged. "Do the bosses ever tell us minions what's going on, especially when it comes to their whores?"

"Yeah, I suppose not."

Kane leaned his head slightly out of the window, lowering his voice. "Listen, you wouldn't believe how expensive this one is. Your boss must be really frustrated and in need of someone to help him work off some stress."

The man's head bobbed. "It's been one hell of a night."

Kane gestured toward the gate. "Well then, we better get her in there before he decides to take his frustrations out in some other way and somebody gets hurt."

The man pursed his lips and stared at his partner. "What do you think?"

The man shrugged. "Our orders were to not let anyone in except our people."

Kane raised his hand slightly. "Hey, if those are your orders, then I understand. I'll let Mr. Lavrov know that his gift was refused at the gate. I wouldn't want him to think that Mr. Novak was ungrateful."

This got a reaction out of both men.

"Wait a minute, you didn't say she was a gift from Mr. Lavrov."

"Didn't I?"

The man shook his head vehemently.

"Sorry about that. I guess I hadn't felt it was necessary since only someone extremely well-connected would know that Mr. Novak is here and in need of a gift." Kane put the car in reverse, the backup lights illuminating the pavement behind him, the sun having set over an hour ago. "I'll let Mr. Lavrov know." He eased up on the brake and the car rolled backward. The guard held up a hand, his eyes bulging.

"No, wait!"

Kane pressed on the brake. "What?"

"You're right. Almost nobody knows that Mr. Novak is here." He jerked his head toward the guard house and the second man, equally flustered, headed inside. The gate rolled open a moment later and the second guard reappeared.

Kane put the car in Drive and smiled at the man. "I think you just saved all of our asses. My boss might not have blamed yours, but he probably would have insisted I had screwed up somehow." They pulled through the gate and slowly made their way toward the main house as he rolled up his window. He glanced in the rearview mirror at Sherrie. "That wasn't too hard."

"Speak for yourself. The underwire in this thing is digging into me like nobody's business. You realize how hard it is to smile for that long when you're in pain?"

Kane grinned. "You could always take it off."

"I could, but if Chris found out, he'd probably think I was an exhibitionist."

"Aren't you?"

She winked. "Of course, but he doesn't need to know all my dirty secrets."

Kane laughed and checked the mirror to see the gate slowly close behind them, the cue for the next part of the operation.

This better work.

Dawson spotted the well-lit main gate as they rounded the bend on the one-four corner of the estate. Kane and Sherrie were on the grounds with no suspicions raised, and so far, everything was going according to plan. "Cross your fingers," he said to Red as he sent the signal. "This is Zero-One. Execute."

Leroux replied, "Executing."

Dawson smiled, exchanging fist bumps with Red as the estate fell dark, emergency lighting kicking in a moment later, leaving the gate stalled in the open position.

"Taking out the generator," came Niner's voice over the comms, and a moment later the thunderclap from the sniper rifle was followed by most of the emergency lighting going dim or completely out as they switched to their own internal batteries. "Taking out the guards." Two more shots sounded, almost in unison, and the guards at the front gate dropped in heaps as Red pulled up.

Dawson smiled, everything still going as planned. "This is it, people. Eliminate anyone with a weapon, but save Maxim for Spock and I."

Spock reached forward from the rear seat and gave Dawson's shoulder a squeeze. "Amen, brother."

"Execute Phase Two."

Atlas immediately replied. "Zero-Seven repositioning, ETA at gate two minutes, over."

Red pulled through the gate with the headlights out as Dawson wondered how many would survive, if he'd ever see home again, or if this truly was it. Right now, he didn't care if he lived or died, though that was a selfish attitude. Lives depended on him. If he let himself get killed by not being careful, he might not be there to take out the gunman who might get the drop on one of his men.

He squeezed his eyes shut and held his breath. He had to get a grip. This wasn't a suicide mission. They were about to go on a rampage, killing as many Russian scum as they could, but it didn't mean they should abandon all discipline, for if they did, not only could they get themselves killed, but the mission could fail.

And failing to execute Maxim was not an option.

There would be no lengthy interrogation. He only wanted one thing out of the man besides his life—Maggie's body. She deserved a proper burial back home, not some unceremonious body dump in the country of the man who killed her.

"They're entering now," reported Niner.

Dawson looked up to see Kane and his phenomenally sexy partner-in-crime passing through the front door as Red continued to roll them forward slowly. Muzzle flashes silhouetted the doorframe.

"I think they know we're here," said Red as he hammered hard on the gas.

243

Dawson rolled his window down as he drew his side arm, the rapid thuds of multiple weapons firing on the other side of the now-closed door pegging his concern for Kane and Sherrie. Red slammed on the brakes, the ABS shuddering them to a halt as all four doors were thrown open. Dawson sprinted toward the entrance.

"This is Zero-One. Making entry now."

Kane replied immediately. "Break left upon entry. Providing cover fire now."

Heavier fire erupted as Dawson acknowledged the instructions. He shoved open the door and broke left at a crouch, his head on a swivel as he took in the scene. A large staircase was ahead of him, the wide steps tapering as they rose, then widening again near the top where a large space on the second floor provided the enemy with a clear view of everything below. At least two gun positions were active overhead, with two more firing from a room to the left.

Dawson scurried toward Kane and Sherrie's position, which appeared to be a large closet, the thick stone walls used in the construction revealed by the bullet holes torn through the wood paneling. "This is Zero-One. Hold outside, over."

"Copy that," responded Red.

Kane glanced at him. "Nice of you to join us. You didn't happen to bring any party favors?"

Dawson pulled two grenades off his belt, handing one to Kane, the other to Sherrie. "You plan on fighting in your underwear the entire time?"

She shrugged. "It gives me freedom of movement."

"Uh-huh." Dawson holstered his sidearm then handed a flashbang to Sherrie. "Grenades up top, flashbang around the corner. I'll provide cover." The two CIA operatives nodded and readied themselves as Dawson unslung his submachine gun. "Ready?"

"Ready," replied Kane and Sherrie.

He leaned out, squeezing the trigger, the weapon set to full auto, 9x19 millimeter rounds spraying across the upper level. "Now!"

Kane leaned out and tossed his grenade then ducked back behind their cover as Sherrie did the same. The flashbang switched hands and she leaned out a second time as Dawson continued the suppression fire. She whipped it around the corner then crouched back behind Kane as Dawson took cover.

Kane's grenade went off first and someone above cried out. It was quickly followed by Sherrie's, and a moment later the flashbang. Dawson rushed forward and around the corner. A man was grabbing his ears, his weapon on the floor at his feet. Dawson put two rounds into him as his head spun to the right, searching for the second position. He didn't see him, but there was a couch pockmarked with bullet holes that likely came from Kane or Sherrie on their initial entry. He squeezed the trigger, sending a spray of lead through the couch. Someone groaned. Dawson quickly rounded the furniture, putting another bullet in the man as he reached for his gun. Dawson made certain no one else was in the room as several bursts of gunfire erupted upstairs.

"Clear!" yelled Kane quickly followed by Sherrie echoing the same.

Dawson shouted the all-clear and activated his comms. "This is Zero-One. Entry is clear, over."

A string of copies was heard and moments later Red, Spock, and Jagger entered.

"You two good?" asked Dawson as he peered up the stairs.

Kane appeared giving a thumbs-up, then Sherrie.

"You two clear upstairs. Spock and I will do the main floor. Red and Jagger hold the main entrance, and watch the outside."

Everyone acknowledged the orders as Dawson broke left with Spock, heading deeper into the house. Gunfire rang out overhead. Two short bursts. Kane's voice came in over the comms a moment later.

"This is Chunky-Monkey. We're okay, continuing to clear, over."

"Copy that," replied Dawson as Spock pulled open a door. Dawson entered, breaking left, hugging the wall as Spock did the same on the right, quickly confirming what appeared to be a large dining room was empty. A set of swinging doors at the far end on the right suggested a kitchen substantial enough to feed all those who might sit around the massive table. They continued toward the door in silence, taking up position on either side of it. The thunderclap of a sniper rifle broke the silence, quickly followed by two more shots.

Niner reported. "This is One-One. Three targets down. They came from what appears to be a guest house. No sign of further activity, over."

Dawson didn't acknowledge the report, instead maintaining their silence as he exchanged hand signals with Spock. Dawson reached out with his arm and gently pushed on one of the doors. It swung in a couple of inches, creaking loudly. Gunfire responded and he jerked back as bullets pierced the wood. He indicated for a flashbang and Spock pulled one off his belt, yanking the pin. He pushed the door open on his side with his boot and tossed it in. They both covered their ears as the device detonated. Screams from its victims rang out and they both shoved the doors aside, rapidly entering, their weapons spitting at anything armed that moved. Three more targets were down when Dawson spotted a chef's hat moving behind a counter.

"Hold your fire," he ordered, and Spock checked his weapon. Dawson switched to Russian. "Let me see your hands!"

Three kitchen staff slowly rose.

"Where's your boss?"

The three exchanged glances but said nothing.

Dawson aimed his weapon at the man with the biggest hat. "Where is he?"

"Which-which one?" His voice was aquiver, the man clearly terrified. This wasn't a mobster, this was a chef who fed mobsters. Dawson's mind couldn't help but wander to The Big Bang Theory and the menu with 'mobster sauce.'

"Maxim might just be a guest," whispered Spock. "They might not think of him as the boss."

Spock was right. Dawson tried a different tack. "Maxim Novak. He arrived here with some of his people in the past couple of hours. Where is he?"

The man shook his head rapidly. "I don't know, I didn't see anyone. But I know they have a special room in the basement where they take people they don't want us to see."

"Where in the basement?"

A shaky hand pointed to the left at a door. "Through there. There's a door on the left. That's the stairs to the basement. They bring people through the side door they don't want us to see. I don't know where in the basement. I've never been there. We're not allowed."

"It's forbidden," said one of the other staff members, her hat tilted to the side revealing short, bright pink hair. "None of us have been there."

Dawson headed for the door in question. "You three, stay put. Make sure your hands stay up or you could get shot."

Three heads nodded, six hands shot higher.

Dawson activated his comms. "This is Zero-One. Three staff members in the kitchen have indicated there's a location in the basement where they take people they don't want the staff to see." He pushed through the door and into the hall, spotting the side entrance on the right and a door opposite. "We're making entry now. Chunky-Monkey, status?"

"Second floor cleared. Returning to main entrance."

"Copy that. Zero-Two and Zero-Eight, join us through the room on your left. Go through the dining room then through the kitchen. There are three staff members in there unarmed. They'll tell you where to go."

"Copy that," responded Red.

Dawson twisted the knob to the door to the basement, then carefully opened it several inches. The hinges glided quietly, the door evidently well-maintained so as not to reveal to the staff when someone was coming or going. He listened but heard nothing. He pulled the door all the way open, the hinges remaining silent, and peered into the darkness, still hearing nothing. He pulled the flashlight off his belt and flicked it on, bathing the stairs in light. He searched for any booby traps then took a tentative step.

The stairs didn't creak, much to his relief. He continued forward with his sidearm in one hand, the flashlight in the other, and as he pushed forward in silence, Spock remained in the doorway, waiting for the others to join them to cover their rear. Two mouth clicks behind him sounded and he glanced up to see Spock coming down the steps, Red and Jagger now covering the door. Dawson continued forward and spotted a faint light ahead. He did one last check for tripwires, then snapped off his light before swiftly covering the remaining steps, emerging into what appeared to be a large lounge. The dim light was coming from a wet-bar at the far end, and some strip lighting hidden

248

under a drink rail surrounding most of the couches and chairs strategically placed throughout the space.

Spock broke right as Dawson took left, and they quickly confirmed the room was empty. Spock pointed at a door near his position, the only way out of the room besides the stairs leading up. The estate they were in was large, and though big, this rec room didn't account for the entire basement. Dawson joined Spock, who yanked open the door. Dawson peered around the corner, finding a long corridor with at least half a dozen doors along the inner wall. All were closed, the only thing distinguishing them from each other was numbers over each. His thoughts immediately went to sex trafficking. Behind each door was likely a bedroom occupied by someone either on the payroll or involuntarily there. A pit formed in his stomach as he imagined Maggie held as one of their sex slaves, forced to entertain members of the mob and their guests.

He held his ear to the first door but heard nothing. Spock took up a covering position as Dawson tried the doorknob. It turned, and he threw it open, Spock stepping inside first, Dawson following. His stomach sank as his suspicion was confirmed. A large bed sat against the far wall, covered in bright red satin sheets, gaudy decorations adorning the room.

Spock shook his head. "Best Little Whorehouse in Moscow?"

Dawson grunted. "I don't think we'll be seeing Dolly Parton any time soon."

Spock pointed at the door. "Notice anything?"

Dawson peered at it, shaking his head. "What am I looking at?"

"It locks from the outside."

Dawson's head slowly bobbed. He pointed at an intercom panel on the wall. "That must be how they ask to be let out."

Spock scratched the back of his neck. "If I'm here and I've just defiled some woman that I'm going to burn in Hell for, I press the button to tell them I'm ready to leave. I don't want to be hanging around here for very long."

Dawson smiled slightly as he picked up on what Spock was getting at. "Which means the other end of this panel is very close."

Spock jabbed a finger at it. "Find the other end, and we may be able to listen in on the rooms."

Dawson headed for the door. "Let's find it." He pointed in the direction they had come from. "You go that way. It could be in the lounge. I'm guessing behind the bar. I'll go this way."

Spock headed swiftly toward the door leading to the lounge as Dawson continued deeper into the den of iniquity. As he passed the door with the number four on it, there was a whimper on the other side, a whimper he had little doubt was from a woman. He stopped and pressed his ear against the door. There was no denying somebody was on the other side, that it was a woman, and that she was crying.

His gut told him whoever was on the other side of the door was alone. If Maxim were with her, he'd be demanding she remain quiet. A moment of indecision gripped him. If Maxim wasn't inside, where was he? The house had been cleared, though there could be a hidden panic room they might never find. Not in the time they had. He clenched his jaw. He was here to kill Maxim, not save people. When he accomplished his primary mission, then he could turn his attention to the man's victims.

The woman whimpered again and he closed his eyes as he struggled to ignore the innocent suffering on the opposite side of the door, suffering he could end by merely letting her know her rescue was at hand. He reached for the doorknob and gripped it, then stopped. What would her reaction be? She might scream when he stepped inside, or she might cower in fear then cry out with joy when she found out she was rescued. Either one would reveal he was there, and he was convinced Maxim was here, somewhere in this basement.

His comms crackled. "I found the panel. Somebody is in rooms four and six."

Dawson stepped over to room five, pressed an ear against the door, finding it silent, then headed for six. He gripped his sidearm tightly, then flexed his fingers. As he leaned closer to the door, he could hear talking, though not what was said. But the fact it sounded like there were two different voices had him convinced this was where his target was. The question was who he was talking to, for it made all the difference in how they entered the room.

If it was one of Maxim's henchmen, they could enter and just kill anything in a spray of bullets. Mission accomplished. But if he was speaking to one of his victims, to one of the women he held prisoner here, they had to enter more cautiously.

And if Maxim were as desperate as Dawson suspected he was, he was likely using whoever was in there with him as a human shield, perhaps with a gun pressed to their head. Nothing he hadn't dealt with before, but it changed the variables.

Spock reentered the hallway, beckoning him away from the door. Dawson joined him farther down the hall. "Definitely two people in there, a man and a woman."

Dawson pursed his lips for a moment. "Could you make out what they were saying?"

"No, it was all whispers, and mostly him. She barely said anything, but…" His friend hesitated.

"But what?"

Spock leaned in closer. "I don't want to get your hopes up, buddy, but I swear it sounded like Maggie."

Maggie lay on the bed, spreadeagle, her hands and feet tied to the four corners by leather straps there when they arrived. The little bit of the room she could make out through her swollen eyes suggested this was some sort of torture chamber, though not for interrogation. The questions had stopped after what had happened earlier. She had heard her beloved's voice and had wanted to cry out to him, to let him know she was alive, but she had resisted the urge and instead let the negotiation play out. It was obvious she was supposed to be part of a hostage exchange, but something had gone wrong. Two shots had been fired at her, and when she felt no pain, she decided playing dead was the best option in case the shooter wasn't aware he had missed. When they had made their escape, it was evident the man had missed intentionally, the words spat at her chilling her to her core.

"If you thought you suffered before, you were sadly mistaken."

She had curled up into a ball and sobbed quietly until they arrived at their destination, where she was hauled from the vehicle and into a building, the hood covering her face revealing little. When she had been strapped to the bed, she realized the suffering the man had in mind. The beatings were over. Now they intended to rape her, most likely repeatedly, most likely for years. She might be trafficked around the world. She had to figure out a way to kill herself, though how that was even possible, she did not know.

When gunfire erupted overhead shortly after they arrived, her hope was renewed. It had to be her fiancé and their friends, or the authorities. Either way, there was hope of rescue. But when the gunfire stopped and nobody came, that hope had begun to wane. In the silence, her captor had started to pace. She could see his shadow move left to right at the foot of the bed, muttering to himself, occasionally reminding her of what he had planned for her. And as the silence continued, she lost all hope.

The gunfire she had heard followed by explosions suggested a violent battle. She couldn't imagine that Dawson was able to come here with many of the others, and she had no idea how many Russians were at this location. They could have been hopelessly outnumbered and died in a desperate attempt to rescue her. It broke her heart, and she sobbed anew as she mourned the man she loved and their friends who would have followed him through the gates of Hell without him asking. She cried out at the thought of their families without a father, without a husband, without a son, without a brother. When a soldier died, the ruin it left behind stretched far and wide, and was felt for a lifetime. And these men wouldn't have died in combat for their country, but instead died in an attempt to save her. It meant no honors. It meant no burial in Arlington.

"Be quiet!" snapped her captor.

"Why don't you go to hell!" she spat back. "Just kill me and get it over with!"

"I said quiet!" The shadow at the front of the bed was now beside her, the mattress shifting as he sat beside her, the cool metal of a gun's muzzle pressing against her temple. "Keep your mouth shut, or I'll blow your head off," he hissed.

She suppressed a smile as he promised the out she so desperately wanted. "Why? Are you afraid that all your men are dead? That my fiancé has killed them all? When he finds you, you're going to regret every finger you laid on me." She drew a deep breath. "BD, I'm in here!"

It was a weak effort, her cracked ribs leaving little air behind her cry, but she wasn't aiming to be heard. Her only goal was to strike the fear of discovery in her captor. She wanted him to pull the trigger, she wanted him to silence her forever, to put an end to this nightmare she was now living.

And to preempt an even more horrifying one.

The hard muzzle pressed deeper into her flesh. "I said shut up!"

"You're never going to shut me up. He's going to find you, he's going to kill you, and he's going to do it slowly."

"That's it, bitch! You're dead!"

Spock gripped Dawson's arm, stopping him from rushing headlong into the room. Maggie's desperate cries were heartbreaking, and he could only imagine how painful it must be for his friend to hear the woman he loved so terrified. He pulled him back from the door. "She's alive. Now let's keep her that way."

Dawson drew a breath and held it, then finally nodded. "You're in charge."

Spock felt the door, giving it a gentle push. It didn't feel substantial, and the fact they could hear Maggie and Maxim on the other side of the door further confirmed that its construction was no different than the other doors they had seen.

"I'll breach. You go in and take left, I'll take right."

Dawson agreed then took a step back, his Grach gripped in both hands, extended in front of him. He nodded at Spock. "Let's do this."

This was probably the most critical breach of Spock's career, and the pressure threatened to overwhelm him. On the opposite side of that door was a woman the entire team cared about long before Dawson had started dating her, a woman even he had thought was dead, his suggestion she might still be alive merely prudence rather than hope. Now, if they handled things properly, they had a chance of saving her, of bringing back a life they all thought they had lost.

Yet he was also torn. On the other side of that door was Maxim, the man responsible for the death of his wife. To save Maggie, they had to kill him, and they had to do it efficiently and effectively. His desire had been to kill the man slowly, to let him suffer, but unfortunately circumstances were denying him that pleasure. Instead, he would have to be satisfied that the man was dead. And that Maggie was safe.

"That's it, bitch! You're dead!"

Spock's heart raced at the screamed threat. He stepped back then lunged forward, raising his right boot and kicking the door. The flimsy lock shattered and the door flew aside. Dawson darted past him on his left, his weapon raised, and Spock surged in after him, scanning to the right. Maggie lay tied to the bed with Maxim sitting beside her, a pistol whipping toward them. Spock squeezed the trigger of his Grach and continued to squeeze it, Dawson doing the same beside him as bullet after bullet hammered the man's chest, his entire body shaking as Maggie squeezed her swollen eyes shut and screamed.

They both emptied their mags then Dawson rushed forward, grabbed Maxim's twitching corpse, and tossed him to the floor. He holstered his weapon then drew his knife, hurrying around the bed, cutting the bindings that held his fiancée. Spock reloaded and straddled Maxim, who stared back up at him, the life fading from his eyes. Spock aimed his weapon directly at the man's head. "This is for my wife." He emptied another mag into the vermin's skull, leaving nothing but a bloody pulp.

Spock closed his eyes as the tears flowed and his head slumped onto his chest.

I miss you, baby.

Dawson stared down at the woman he loved, her face barely recognizable from what had happened to her. He gently stroked her hair as her screams of terror turned into sobs of relief the moment her ties were cut.

"BD, is that you?" Her voice was weak, a shadow of what it should be, the vigor he was so accustomed to hearing beaten down. Her cries for help must have been exhausting, if the wheezing in her chest was any indication.

"It's me. You're safe now."

Her sobs resumed and she reached up for him. He leaned over her, careful not to put any of his weight on her, and gently embraced her.

"I'm so sorry," she whispered in his ear. "I had to tell them. I couldn't take the pain anymore."

He stroked her head, tears flowing at her words. "It's okay. Nobody blames you."

"Is everyone all right?"

"Joanne died."

Maggie gasped and Spock whimpered behind him.

"Is that Spock?" she asked.

"Yes."

"Spock, I'm sorry. Can you ever forgive me?"

Spock sniffed. "It wasn't your fault, Maggie. She was dead before she even got to the hospital, long before you told them anything." He left the room and

Dawson heard him radioing in the status, and moments later heavy footfalls echoed down the hallway as Jagger and Red joined them.

Dawson gave Maggie a gentle kiss. "Shirley and Vanessa are fine. The entire team is fine. Thankfully, Joanne was the only casualty." He stroked her hair again. "How did you know we were in the hallway?"

Tears rolled. "I didn't."

"But you were calling my name."

She turned her head away, as if the words she was about to speak were too shameful. "I wanted to die. I wanted him to get so angry he would kill me. I thought you were all dead. When the gunfire stopped, I thought they were going to…"

"Shhh," said Dawson. "I understand."

Red stepped inside the room and gasped. He gently took Dawson by the shoulders and pulled him away as Jagger moved in with a medkit and quickly began assessing Maggie. "We need to get her out of here fast," said Red. "We could have reinforcements coming down on us at any moment."

Dawson nodded, unable to tear his eyes away as Jagger completed his assessment. "Several cracked, perhaps broken ribs, possible internal bleeding, extensive bruising to the stomach, chest, and face."

"Can you give her something for the pain?"

Jagger shook his head. "Not yet. I need to do a better assessment. We need to get her out of here now. I recommend we take her to the nearest hospital."

Dawson nodded. "Let's do it. I'll go in with her. I want the rest of you to get home as quickly as possible. I'll deal with the fallout."

Red knew better than to argue with him.

"We need a stretcher," said Jagger. "We have to stabilize her."

257

"There's a table in that lounge that should fit the bill," said Spock. "I'll go get it."

Maggie reached out and Dawson took her hand, sitting beside her. "We're going to have you out of here in no time. Just hang in there a little longer."

She nodded, saying nothing.

And as he leaned in to give her another kiss on the forehead, Niner's voice squawked in his ear.

"This is One-One. We might have a problem."

Niner rolled onto his back, his hands up as half a dozen Russian regulars aimed Kalashnikovs at him, removing any doubt on whether they did indeed have a problem. "Hello, gentlemen. Lovely evening for a stroll, isn't it?"

"Get up," ordered one of the men.

Niner rose as ordered. Helicopters roared overhead, racing toward the estate, the thunder of their rotors the first tip-off that something was about to go very wrong. Yet these were Russian military, not Russian mob, and he wasn't sure how he felt about that. The mob, he could just kill and there would be little to no consequences. But the Russian military? They couldn't touch them.

Their mission was over, Dawson's promise to Colonel Clancy to not make the evening news broken. This was going to make international headlines. Their faces would be splashed over screens across the world, effectively ending their careers, assuming they didn't end up in a Russian prison, or exchanged with their government only to serve the rest of their years in Leavenworth. But the news that Maggie was alive and that Maxim was dead made it all worth it. They might all go to prison, their lives might be finished, but she was going to live. And after killing scores of brutal criminals, countless future lives were likely saved as well.

He had no regrets.

As he was led down the hill toward the estate, at least a dozen soldiers swarmed the gate. Atlas threw down his weapons and raised his hands. Niner breathed a sigh of relief that his best friend was making it out of this alive. A few more minutes of walking through the sometimes heavy brush had them at the gate.

He smiled at his friend. "What? Couldn't outrun them?"

Atlas rolled his eyes. "Do you ever shut up?"

"Your life would be empty if I were silent."

"Shut up!" snapped one of the soldiers.

Atlas bowed slightly to the man. "Thank you."

"You're welcome."

Atlas grinned. "Not even five minutes and he's already sick of you," he whispered.

Niner stuck a tongue out at him, not willing to risk a rifle butt to the gut.

"Well, this turned into a Charlie-Foxtrot pretty quickly," said Kane as he peered outside.

Dawson had to agree, though he didn't care. Maggie was alive and Maxim was dead, and he had yet to come down from that high. No one else was dying tonight, though lengthy prison sentences were likely.

He could live with that.

"I better go talk to them."

Kane glanced back at him. "Do you want me to come with you?"

Dawson shook his head, stripping himself of any weapons. "No, it's best just one of us goes."

Kane jerked a thumb at Sherrie, now covered by a robe. "We could send her out."

She flashed them and grinned. "I'll show them these, and you can all escape out the back."

Dawson chuckled. "That's crazy enough it might just work, but I think your assets have been used enough tonight." He stepped through the door, his hands raised, his eyes scanning the situation. Two large Mi-26 Halo heavy transport choppers were on the lawn, an Mi-28NM Havoc attack helicopter overhead. Large lights were aimed at him from multiple directions as he was quickly surrounded, though not detained. No one came within ten yards of him. A silhouette walked toward him, and it wasn't until they were face-to-face that Dawson recognized it was Minister Novak.

"So, we meet at last, face-to-face, so to speak," said the man.

Dawson bowed his head. "Yes, sir."

"Your fiancée?"

"Alive, though for how long, I'm not certain. She requires immediate medical attention."

"I suspected that might be the case, so, if you will permit me…"

There was no point in denying any requests the man might make. Dawson nodded and the minister motioned with a finger over his shoulder, pointing toward the front entrance. "Medics only!" he shouted in Russian.

Dawson activated his comms. "Everyone lower your weapons. They're sending in medics."

"Copy that," replied Red.

"It's safe for your people to go in, sir."

"Thank you."

Two medics rushed by, carrying several bags of equipment and a stretcher.

"And my son?"

Dawson frowned. "I regret to inform you, sir, that your son is dead."

The minister's head slowly bobbed. "I must admit, I'm sad to hear that, though too much of me is relieved."

"Sir, should it be necessary for someone to answer for what happened here tonight, let it be me. My people were only following my orders."

The minister smirked at him. "Orders? So, you are military?"

Dawson shook his head. "Ex-military. We all resigned before taking the actions we did. The American government and people should not be held responsible for what has happened here today."

The minister regarded him for a moment before delivering the final verdict. "There is only one person who should pay a price for these events, and he already has. You and your men will be disarmed and escorted to the airport where you will depart our country immediately."

Dawson bowed his head again, containing his elation. "Thank you, sir. I recommend you thoroughly search the house. There is at least one woman in the basement that I believe is being held against her will. There may be more."

"I'll have it taken care of."

There was a commotion at the door and Dawson turned to see Red and Jagger carrying Maggie on a stretcher with two Russian medics on either side, one carrying an IV, another radioing in her status.

The minister pointed toward one of the helicopters. "You may go with her."

"Thank you, sir."

Leroux's voice crackled in his ear. "Zero-One, Control. We've been monitoring. If the Russians are going to let you go unmolested, we prepositioned a private jet at Vnukovo International. I recommend your team uses that plane. You'll make it out of Russian air space in an hour. If Maggie is stable enough, we can have the plane land in Warsaw with medical personnel waiting. Total flight time is about two-point-five hours."

Dawson pointed at his ear, addressing the minister's puzzled expression. "I've been informed we have a flight waiting for us at Vnukovo International Airport."

"Then I suggest you take it. *All* of you."

Dawson stared at the stretcher being loaded in the back of one of the helicopters. "She might not be stable enough to fly for several hours."

"That might not matter. I can't guarantee your safety. All I can promise is that you won't be arrested for what happened, and you'll be allowed to leave when it's safe for your fiancée to do so. But once word gets out about what happened, about my son being killed along with so many others involved with the mafia, somebody could talk, and they won't hesitate to hit any hospital your fiancée may be in. Leave the country now, and nobody will ever know who did this. They'll assume a rival gang, and I will make certain the investigation will indicate the same thing. But if you and your fiancée are in a hospital for a week or two under heavy guard, someone will talk. These people have contacts everywhere."

Dawson beckoned Jagger, and he jogged over from the helicopter now holding Maggie. "It's been suggested that Maggie might not be safe here from reprisals. Can she make it to Warsaw, two-point-five hours?"

Jagger stared back over his shoulder at the helicopter. "I can't guarantee it, but she should. Her vitals are good and the abdominal bruising doesn't appear to be spreading. She's on an IV now so she's getting fluids, and we've got her on oxygen. Assuming they give us supplies, and assuming nothing else goes wrong, then yes, she should make it, but BD, she's in rough shape. The chances of something going wrong aren't slim to none."

The minister stepped closer, lowering his voice so no one else could hear. "There's something you need to know. My son was the *Pakhan*, the boss, of the New York Russian mafia, and he had ambitions, which means he had rivals. My men intercepted a group that was on their way here."

"Rivals?" asked Jagger.

The minister shook his head. "No, these were reinforcements, but now they're all dead. The bodies are being brought here, and everything will be staged to make it appear as if it were rival gangs. Like I said, they won't suspect anything—he had rivals. But you're all loose ends. If you want to stay here with your fiancée, I'll support your decision, but if it's discovered, the entire coverup is blown. If you leave, there's no reason for anyone to question the story."

Dawson pursed his lips as he pondered the situation. He had no illusions that the minister was doing this for their benefit. If Kane's contacts were correct, then the minister had already delivered a story that didn't involve his son. He had lied to his people and was here to put an end to a situation that could affect his career. His plan to stage the crime scene as if it were a rival hit was not spur of the moment. The troops that were here now had to be loyal, had to be hand-picked. If someone talked, it could mean trouble for the minister.

But none of that was his concern. Maggie was. The man was right. If word got out, the Russian mob wouldn't hesitate to kill her in retaliation for the deaths of so many of their own. They had already proven back home that hospitals weren't sacred territory, and here they would likely have help from the inside.

They had no choice.

Dawson decided. "We're taking the flight. All of us." He turned to Jagger. "Make sure you've got everything you're going to need to take care of her."

Jagger snapped out a nod then sprinted back toward the helicopter. Dawson extended a hand to the minister. "Thank you, sir."

The minister clasped both of his hands around Dawson's. "You have my sincerest apologies for what has happened to your fiancée. I pray she makes a speedy recovery."

"Thank you, sir." Dawson headed back into the house where the others were waiting. "Leroux has arranged a flight for us. The Russians are going to take us there now, then we're going to land in Warsaw and offload Maggie to a hospital there."

Kane frowned. "Is she stable enough?"

"We have to take that chance. Jagger says as long as nothing else goes wrong, she should make it, but it's been made clear to me that if she remains here, she may be in more danger. Dump all your gear. We don't want anything that might set off one of those troops out there." He headed back outside and strolled swiftly toward the helicopter and Maggie, praying he was making the right choice.

Approaching Fayetteville Regional Airport

Fayetteville, North Carolina

Dawson held up the tablet so Maggie could see it, the footage Kane had just sent him showing the estate outside Moscow engulfed in flames, a Russian news report narrating the scene.

"I don't remember there being any fire," said Maggie, leaning in.

"There wasn't."

"I guess the minister had them set it on fire to help with the coverup?"

"That would be my guess." He shook the tablet. "Dylan says he thinks the car spontaneously blew up and set the place on fire."

Maggie stared at him, puzzled. "Why would the car blow up?"

Dawson chuckled. "You didn't see what make it was, did you?"

She pointed at her eyes. "I wasn't seeing much."

His chest ached and he leaned in, giving her a gentle peck on the forehead. "Sorry, babe, I forgot."

"So, why would—"

The flight attendant interrupted them. "We're about to land."

Maggie smiled at her. "Thank you."

The young woman collected their drinks and Dawson tightened his lap belt as their descent began. They landed in silence, Maggie leaning against him, her head resting on his shoulder as he stared out the window of the private jet, the last penny of the op financed by their professor friends. When this was all over, they would both be sending the Actons a huge thank you, he was sure.

They landed without incident, and Dawson descended the few steps from the private jet to the tarmac. He held out a hand and helped Maggie down, then breathed a sigh of relief.

They had made it.

They had all made it.

Everything had gone smoothly. Minister Novak had been true to his word. The helicopter had taken them all to the airport, and the professors' private jet was waiting for them as arranged by Leroux. They had departed immediately and landed in Warsaw less than three hours later, where an ambulance took Maggie directly to the hospital. Thankfully, there had been no surprises on the flight, and Jagger had kept her alive.

Dawson had remained with Maggie while the others continued home. Red had informed him that Clancy had torn up the letters of resignation in front of him. It had taken five days before the doctor said it was safe for Maggie to make the flight home. She was much improved, though it would take weeks before she would physically recover, and he feared years for the emotional scars to heal, if they ever did.

A police siren sounded, just two squawks to draw attention. An unmarked car pulled up, the four detectives working the case climbing out. Dawson bristled.

Detective Samuel smiled at them both. "Sergeant Major, I presume this is the missing Maggie Harris?"

Maggie took Dawson's arm, wrapping hers around it as she leaned against him. "I am."

"I had to see for myself that it was indeed you."

"Does this close your case?" asked Dawson.

Samuel smirked. "This is the FBI's case now. As far as the Fayetteville Police Department is concerned, there is no case anymore. I'm just happy to see that you're safe and well, Miss Harris. I would expect you'll get a visit from the FBI shortly." He leaned closer to Dawson, lowering his voice. "I would suggest that you not mention what route you took to Warsaw, especially if that happened to take you through New York City. Or Moscow."

Dawson smiled slightly. "I couldn't tell you the last time I've been to New York City."

Samuel chuckled. "I'm sure you can't." He extended a hand and Dawson shook it. "Good luck, Sergeant Major. And to you, Miss Harris." He shook her hand then headed back toward his car.

Detective Sneider walked over to them, his partner cursing as she scurried to join him. Dawson clenched his fists, Atlas having filled him in on their encounter. Sneider leaned in, lowering his voice. "Listen, we're all pretty sure what you guys did, and while officially we can't condone it, I think it's effin' spectacular. While I'll never be a fan of the military, I'm a big fan of what you guys did in New York and what I suspect you did in Moscow." He extended a hand and Dawson took it. "Tell your friend that I'm sorry for giving him a hard time."

"I will."

Sneider let go of his hand then flashed a smile at Maggie before heading back to the car, his partner relieved, quickly shaking both their hands before joining her colleagues.

The unmarked car left, and Dawson and Maggie headed for the private terminal. As they approached, the door was hauled open by a grinning Niner. "Welcome home!"

They entered and cheers erupted, all of Bravo Team and their partners, including the colonel, celebrating their safe return. Clancy walked up and shook Maggie's hand, giving her a kiss on each cheek.

"I'm so pleased to see you're all right."

"Thank you, sir."

Clancy shook Dawson's hand. "Thank you for keeping your faces off the news."

"We tried our best, sir."

"You'll be happy to know that the American Embassy in Moscow reported that the official investigation into Maxim's death concluded it was a rival gang that killed him and his people to prevent him from moving in on their turf."

Maggie stared up at Dawson. "Then it's over?"

He smiled at her reassuredly. "It appears so."

Clancy patted them each on the shoulder. "Miss Harris, take as much time as you need. Sergeant Major, I'll see you next Monday."

"Yes, sir."

Clancy turned and headed out of the terminal, his departure the signal for everyone else to swarm. And as the reunion kicked into full swing, he took a step back, reflecting on what had happened over the past week. Joanne was dead. Maggie would recover physically, but along with Shirley and Vanessa, would be scarred for life over what had happened.

What his team had done in response was legally wrong. They had killed dozens of people, broken countless laws, but as he watched Maggie smiling and laughing, surrounded by her friends, and he enjoyed the camaraderie of his brothers in arms, he knew there was only one answer to the question of whether he would do it all again.

In a heartbeat.

THE END

ACKNOWLEDGMENTS

It has been a brutal five months that included three surgeries, dozens of hours in the ER, scores of visits to the wound clinic, countless appointments with doctors and specialists, weeks of non-stop pain pegged at level 9-10, a serious risk of death, and events that I will never forget.

While I suffered, I experienced a medical system at its breaking point, people going through far worse than I who exhibited incredible bravery, and the soul-crushing sounds as ER personnel tried, and failed, to save a man's life within earshot of me.

I suffered through doctors who didn't want to operate, some scared to operate, and some who mistakenly thought they weren't supposed to. Thankfully, I also had nurses who, despite being exhausted, were always supportive and pleasant, some of whom questioned the doctors' diagnosis, and ultimately proved to be correct.

And I had one dermatologist who had the courage to operate without hesitation, leading to my current status of almost recovered. She also discovered I had picked up a dangerous infection, likely in the ER or during aftercare. This infection could have killed me if it had spread to my bloodstream, but I am now on the mend, and, fingers crossed, am no longer in danger.

This isn't over, but my suffering is. It is now more of an inconvenience, but I was finally able to write again, and this book is the result. As you can see, I took my frustrations out on the Russian mob.

It was fun.

As usual, there are people to thank. My dad for all the research, Brent Richards for some weapons info, Greg "Chief" Michael for some general US Army info, and, as always, my wife, daughter, my late mother who will always be an angel on my shoulder as I write, as well as my friends for their continued support, and my fantastic proofreading team! As well, I'd like to thank my Facebook followers for some character name suggestions, including Deanna Blackshire, Charlene Klasen, Mark Gilliard, Travis Galceran, and Lindy Jones Zywot.

To those who have not already done so, please visit my website at www.jrobertkennedy.com, then sign up for the Insider's Club to be notified of new book releases. Your email address will never be shared or sold.

Thank you once again for reading.

Made in the USA
Middletown, DE
11 February 2023

24633726R00168